MAX DANIELS

THE SPACE GUARDIAN

P
A KANGAROO BOOK
PUBLISHED BY POCKET BOOKS NEW YORK

Another *Original* Publication of POCKET BOOKS

POCKET BOOKS, a Simon & Schuster division of
GULF & WESTERN CORPORATION
1230 Avenue of the Americas, New York, N.Y. 10020

ISBN: 0-671-81888-0

First Pocket Books printing August, 1978

Trademarks registered in the United States and other countries.

Printed in the U.S.A.

THE SPACE
GUARDIAN

Chapter

1

"Very well, Mhoss, the jest has gone far enough. Rumors buzz. The staff wonders. Even your most accustomed companions are shocked. Now thumb the cancellation of your withdrawal from the Institute."

Twelve cold gray eyes of the Guardian Institute's Director glared into the mild brown ones of a very attractive humanoid female. That glare, shining out of the coal-black gleaming face, had been known to throw strong beings into convulsions, but it had no more effect on Lahks Mhoss than to start a twinkle in her eyes. Nonetheless, her face remained grave and her voice was even a little sad as she replied.

"It is no jest. I have said so over and over. It is my right to withdraw at any time up to the final imprinting. I choose to withdraw, Director."

"Why? You state no reason."

"The form gives reason as optional. I prefer not to state mine."

"People who do things without reason can be considered irrational and psyched."

Lahks shook her head; her long, straight black hair swung gently, caressing coffee-satin cheeks. "You have my psych reports. They are of public record. To refuse to state a reason is not the same as not having one." The twinkle in her eyes deepened and the corners of a generous mouth twitched a little, as if they were tired of unnatural gravity and sought their normal smiling shape. "Besides, you would not want it known that an irrational individual could proceed so far in the Institute's course—would you?"

Neither the glare nor the expression of the Director changed, but a faceted ring on his many-fingered left hand glittered suddenly, indicating an infinitesimal movement. He did not see the flicker of Lahks' eyes pick up the sign, but he knew she had seen. She missed nothing; in fact, she was one of the finest products of the Institute—except for her warped sense of humor, her passion for practical jokes, and an apparent desire to keep everyone in a constant state of turmoil. The Director was swept with an emotion he had not felt since his own children (now grandfathers) had been very small; that jerk of the hand had been the vestigial remains of a strong impulse to deliver a spanking. In fact, if it had not been for the psych reports Lahks had just mentioned, her penchant for nonsense would have catapulted her out of the Institute in the first few weeks.

Those reports indicated that the principles of the Guardians that needed to be painfully instilled into others were a deep-seated instinct in Lahks Mhoss. She was so suitable for the purposes of the Institute that faults for which others would have been expelled were punished in Lahks by disciplinary measures. Had that been a mistake, the Director wondered? Of course, there was also the fact that she was Ghrey Mhoss' daughter. Then, picking up the conversation without apparent pause, he spoke with cold deliberation.

"And your father, what will he think of this extraordinary behavior?"

Red flickered briefly behind the brown of Lahks' eyes. She shrugged shapely shoulders. "He will think that I had an excellent purpose."

For the first time since she had entered the room, all the Director's eyes moved away from her face. "What do you know about your father, Mhoss?"

"I know that he still is," she snapped, her voice as brittle as untempered glass, "which is more than you know."

"How do you know?"

"I am my mother's daughter."

And when the Director looked up from his brief contempla-

8

tion of the single jewel he wore, he was gazing at a pallid albino. Only the faint pink of eyes and lips gave color to skin and hair of translucent whiteness.

"So!" Not a single eye flickered.

First round to me, second to you, Lahks thought.

"Your reasons are easy enough to perceive," he continued, "but your logic is at fault. Do you think it will be easier to find Ghrey yourself than with the full strength of the Guardians behind you?"

Abandoning any effort at sobriety, Lahks laughed. The warm chortle was so intimate and carried so strong an invitation to share amusement that the discipline of a lifetime was strained to preserve the Director's gravity. His hand twitched again.

"Certainly," Lahks replied in a delighted gurgle. "Safer, too." Pert silver curls bobbed against her forehead. Her mood changed abruptly and she leaned forward, saying earnestly, "That is literal truth. Even if you did not send me on some harebrained cosmic wild-goose chase as soon as I was imprinted—which I would lay heartstones against hair-rings you would—as long as I do not have the final imprinting, no key information can be obtained from me, nor am I conditioned to death-by-will. If I should be trapped and taken, they can drug me to the ears, brain-probe me—anything. I cannot be a danger to the Guardians because I do not know anything important. I will be safer because both drug and machine will proclaim my ignorance."

"You think such alternatives preferable to death?"

"Anything is preferable to death. An emptied mind can be refilled. A damaged brain can be repaired. Besides, I do not intend to be caught."

"By whom?"

The question was most casually asked, but Lahks did not fall into the trap. Her laughter gurgled out again while she shook her head.

"I do not know. If I knew, I would tell you—in all truth, I would. This much I promise—if I find where he is and who holds him and it is possible to inform the Institute, I will do so. I like to laugh, but I am not a fool. For rescue missions a strong concerted attack is best. For the seeking of information, one alone is most efficient."

"It is a large universe," the Director said dryly. "If you do not know where to look, where will you begin? Lahks, do you think we have not *been* seeking Ghrey?"

"I will look there." Unerringly, as if drawn by wires, the silver head turned, and the pink eyes stared out toward the rim of the galaxy.

"The rim? Intergalactic space? Another galaxy?"

"I tell you, I do not know." For the first time a hint of impatience shadowed the girl's voice. "I have told you everything I know myself."

"Very well, Lahks. Remember the promise you made. I cannot stop you. We will grant a leave of absence for personal business before final imprinting. Now"—the many-fingered hands folded softly together, belying their strong impulse to wring the pretty neck—"will you tell me why you did not ask for a leave of absence in the first place instead of sending through this withdrawal?"

The warm chortle filled the room again and Lahks leaned forward to plant a resounding kiss above the rows of eyes. "Because it would have been granted and I would not have seen you to say good-bye."

There was a long breath-held silence; all the glowing eyes of the black face closed tight. "That will be ten demerits and a full-period pay loss," the Director said very, very softly. "Remember," he added, in a slightly more natural voice, "that you are a member of the Guardians, and conduct yourself accordingly."

A spurious expression of deep reverence appeared immediately on Lahks' expressive countenance. Once more the Director closed all his eyes and struggled for control. He came of a long-lived race, and in more time than he cared to remember no one had filled him with an equal desire to laugh and commit mayhem at the same time. Eyes still closed, he lifted his hand and pointed the jeweled digit at the door. Lahks giggled, but she turned to go. If she intended to make the shuttle, she had little time to waste.

Grinning broadly, she considered the Director's remark. The years of training in every sophisticated form of physical violence, sedition, and treachery, every method of twisting fact to one's own purpose, in the procedures of bribery, corruption, blackmail, extortion, and mental torture passed through her mind. She wondered mildly as she reached for the door what limits being a member of the Guardians could place on her actions.

Between the time the door hid her from the Director's view and the latch clicked so that the secretary looked up, Lahks had converted hair, skin, and eyes to their original form. Few knew of her mother's people at all; fewer had any real information about them; and if no one at all—except the Director, whom she did not really consider—connected her with those legendary folk, she would be safest of all.

Lahks' goodbyes were already said, and her scanty belongings were in a locker at the port; there was nothing to do but up ship and out. As the acceleration chair gently enfolded her in resilient foam, she thought of the next step. The Institute shuttle would set her down at a major transshipment port. From there she had her choice of hundreds of systems all in the general direction she had to go. Of these, Lahks had chosen the fourth planet of a G-type star called Wumeera. Although it had been colonized by mammalian humanoids early in their star-travel history, it had never developed an elaborate urban civilization because of its inhospitality. The climate alternated between searing deserts and freezing mountains; it offered little in the way of arable land or mineral wealth; there were dust storms that could strip the flesh from the bones and blizzards that could bury one in minutes; and there were dangerous, although unintelligent, natural denizens. Anyone who stayed alive on Wumeera was tough.

Yet, in addition to an indigenous population that had learned to live in its manic conditions, Wumeera attracted a wide range of adventurers. Those who were greedy enough, sly enough, strong enough—or lucky enough—could steal, win, or find a heartstone.

The foam folded back, but Lahks did not move. Other passengers curious to see the stars twist and dance as real space coiled into a new form according to the irresistible logic of mathematics went to the lounge. There viewscreens exposed distance curling into a knot at the command of intelligence. Terra-descended humanoids called the rules, which had bent a straight line into a tight coil that a spaceship could climb like the rungs of a ladder, Carroll's equations. Other races of star jumpers attached different names to the formulas. Regardless of the trivialities of mortal creatures, the equations performed their functions with sublime indifference to the names given them.

Lahks had seen the stars dance often enough, however, to

THE SPACE GUARDIAN

forgo the pleasure in order to pursue her thoughts. The heartstone—it was so much in her mind that she had slipped and mentioned it to the Director. She pushed knowledge of the slip away. He would not interfere with her, but should she delay her prime purpose to obtain one? There were as many legends about the heartstone as about her mother's people, and—Lahks' expressive brows lifted—she did not know the truth about one any more than she knew the truth about the other.

It was possible, Lahks thought, that her mother had never been meant to bear a human child, but she so ordered her body that it performed the feat. Perhaps the sustained strain was too great and she died—but Lahks did not think so. It was more likely that, in spite of her love for Ghrey, Zuhema had gone back to her own people. In any case, before Lahks was old enough to understand the nature of her dual heritage, Zuhema was no longer there to teach her. What Ghrey knew, he kept to himself. Lahks learned from him only that it was necessary always to conceal her inborn abilities. What use she had of them she had learned by private experimentation, and this was what drew her to the heartstone.

One legend among many linked the Changelings to the heartstone. When these two came together, it was rumored, their combined force could alter the universe. Lahks' lips curved up. She did not believe that, but it was possible that possession of the heartstone would unlock the latent powers she knew were in her. Partly she desired that. Power for its own sake meant nothing. But to know you have abilities you cannot use is frustrating. Lahks felt like a cripple who, with mechanical aids, did not need his limbs, but, because walking was his inborn right, desired use of them. If she had a birthright, she wanted use of it.

What the Changelings could do beyond molding their own flesh into any semblance, Lahks did not know. Even in that direction her ability was limited by her human part. She could not change the shape or form of her body except in appearance. She guessed the Changelings, like many other races of the galaxy, had psych power of some kind. Her mother—she remembered that much—had known where she was and what she was doing even when a considerable distance away, and Zuhema could make her presence and desires known to Lahks from afar.

12

What other powers the Changelings had and how these abilities would be altered by her human heritage were questionable.

Lahks was a weak telepathic receiver, but that was not surprising because Ghrey was a Shomir, and telepathy was natural to many of them. And, although Ghrey had no record of telepathic power in his dossier, Lahks had "felt" him after Zuhema was gone. When he was away on the business of the Guardians, a presence, warm and reassuring, kept her from a terrifying sense of aloneness. Even after Ghrey had been declared missing, Lahks remained sure of his existence and sure of his safety. Only in recent months had the sense of presence changed. It had taken on physical direction and a summoning character. There was no urgency in the summoning. Lahks was in no fear as to Ghrey's immediate need, and she had the utmost confidence in the signal—whatever it was. She must come, but there was no hurry. She had time to seek a heartstone if she could use one.

That was the crux of Lahks' immediate problem. She had chosen Wumeera for the type of men who dared its dangers and for its proximity. But the heartstone was there. Ranging in size from a pea to a small egg, the stone had defied analysis by the most sensitive devices. Its chemical composition had, of course, been determined, but that meant as little as saying that man was made up of carbon, oxygen, and hydrogen, with traces of other elements. Instruments that could detect the energy reflected by starlight from the absorptive surface of a dead sun did not react to the heartstone; yet it changed its temperature in one's hand, now warm, now cold. Films sensitive to every range of the visible, infrared, and ultraviolet scales recorded nothing when used to photograph the heartstone—nothing.

Although to the eyes the round or oval stone, dazzling pink to deep red, showed regularly pulsating, coruscating bursts of silver, gold, electric blue, and shocking green within its depth and sometimes rippling over its surface, cameras recorded nothing. No pictorial representation of a heartstone had ever been obtained by mechanical means. Neither the shape of the stone in silhouette nor the background, as if the object were transparent, showed. At all ranges of all radiation, a blurred, irregular blotch with the background dim and distorted was recorded on the film.

So much factual information was stored in the InfoBank; however, it was not the end of the tale. Lahks had scanned what seemed miles of legend, fiction, and personal recounting of experience concerning the heartstone. There were stories of the stones moving by themselves, of their eating away, dissolving, or vaporizing their containers or the surfaces on which they rested—except living organic matter; flesh was never harmed. Indeed, there were legends of heartstones healing wounds and curing illnesses.

The most persistent stories, however, were of symbiotic psychic relationship—at least it was assumed to be symbiotic, because the heartstone's bursts of color became more brilliant, its pulses quicker, its color brighter. What power it conferred on its intelligent symbiont was much in doubt even in legend. And here there was no longer any record of personal experience. Anyone who had entered such a relationship with a heartstone was either totally vague or totally silent. Nonetheless, friends, relatives, and various other onlookers had much to say. Unfortunately, it was very contradictory. One said the heartstone had changed a saint to a monster; another marveled at the alteration of a moody man of barely normal intelligence into a cheerful genius; still another bewailed the slippage of a brilliant, active thinker into a state so dreamy and detached that it was little to be distinguished from idiocy or insanity; finally, there were those who claimed all such tales to be fabrications because they had seen and handled the stones with no response at all.

Lahks stirred restlessly in her seat. Decision could, of course, be delayed until she reached Wumeera and estimated the difficulties and advantages more closely. No sooner had she made the trite observation than she laughed aloud. What a lot of bother to rationalize to herself something she intended from the beginning. No sooner had Wumeera and the heartstone come together in her mind with the legends about her people than she knew she had to have one.

The decision formalized, Lahks leaned back and closed her eyes, trying to open herself wide, to listen with that strange receptor that was neither ears nor mind for her father's sending. It was there, where it always was, emitting alternate or sometimes combined waves of reassurance and beckoning. There was no change, no indication that the decision she had

14

made had been communicated. Unconsciously, Lahks turned her head in the direction of the call. With all the force in her, she tried to send a message back until, after a few moments, she felt the flagging of her energy. Then she listened again.

Almost immediately, certainly in no longer than it would take a person to listen to, consider, and digest an important statement, the answer came: stronger reassurance, which arrived first in a wave that seemed to promise support, then something negative. Lahks tried to reach toward the sending, tried to open her receptivity still further. Disapproval.... No, not that—anxiety; her father was concerned about the dangers she might face, was urging caution, but there was no sense of forbidding. A sensation of loss, a passionate desire to hear Ghrey's voice, swept over Lahks. She sent once more with a burst of energy that drained blood from her face.

"Where are you, Papa? Where?"

And then it seemed to Lahks that she had opened out her very skin into a receiver in her desire to obtain a reply. It came—puzzlement, sorrow, reassurance, beckoning—and on its heels a faint roar, quickly deepening in intensity. For a startled moment Lahks fastened her attention on that sound that was no sound. In the time-space between two heartbeats, she was seized, wrenched a million different ways by the prayers, dreams, hopes of swarms of intelligences.

Lahks did not realize that her physical body had echoed her mental shriek of terror, but an attendant's hand on her shoulder and anxious inquiry helped rescue her from the vortex of need that was sucking at her psyche, threatening to disperse it into atoms once it had a good grip. She shut off everything, even her father's sending, which had become absorbed into that all-encompassing ocean of longing.

"Miss Mhoss, are you ill?"

The tightening grip on her shoulder and the anxious voice snapped her eyes open. "Ill?" she gasped, still dazed.

"Is something wrong? Are you transition-sick?"

"No." The pieces of Lahks' personality seemed to snap together with rubber-band resilience. She had learned something new. She summoned an apologetic half-smile. "It must have been a bad dream."

The attendant looked puzzled. Few people had bad dreams since personality adjustment was so easy, but the universe was large and many strange types inhabited it—especially those who worked at or visited the Guardian Institute. He only asked if he could get Lahks something to help her.

"No, thank you. The effect is ephemeral," she replied. "But you can tell me how long it will be until we make Lyrae Haven. I seem to have lost track of time."

"Fifteen tu, Miss Mhoss."

"Thank you."

Lahks watched the half-raised, gracefully swaying tail of the attendant as it retreated with a frown that had nothing to do with her usual idle puzzlement as to why her particular breed of humanoid had shed such a useful appendage. She was wondering whether she dared open her receptors to her father again. She had not guessed that every living thing that "wanted" sent. Now she realized that she had been trained, perhaps prenatally, to receive on a particular... well, call it wavelength, although the energy sent and received certainly had nothing to do with sound or light. That would be why telepaths born into nontelepathic groups were so frequently insane; there was no one to train them to restrict their reception. But her father... Lahks fought off panic. For the first time in her life she was utterly, completely, alone.

The warning bell rang. People filed back to their seats. Foam enwrapped them. The effects of Carroll's equations were negated. With its customary startling shake, space uncoiled itself and lay flat. Lyrae Haven sent out a slender, probing finger, which the ship grasped firmly. It crawled forward at ten thousand km/tu. The probing finger changed to a softly clasping hand and the ship was pulled gently into its lock. The seat released her; Lahks stood up and defiantly shook out her long black hair. Leading string or no leading string, she would seek out Ghrey. The first phase was finished; now began the second.

Chapter

2

Lahks registered under the number assigned to her as a Guardian trainee at the transient hotel where her reservation had been sent. It was the largest at Lyrae Haven and the busiest. People came and went constantly, sat in the lobby, met friends, asked silly or serious questions at the desk. Nonetheless, the clerk would remember the white teeth that flashed in a smile in the coffee-colored face, would remember the silken swing of long black hair as Lahks asked about ships leaving for Old Terra. There was one the following day. Lahks nodded, passed her Institute card over, and asked that a reservation be made and charged at the trainee rate.

The clerk nodded respectfully and a little regretfully. Guardians, even trainees, were not to be trifled with. He passed the card into the recorder, punched the information, then handed the slip to Lahks to be thumbprinted. That would about wipe out her accumulated back pay, but since Lahks did not plan to be anywhere near where it would be possible to draw upon it, she did not worry. Up in her room, she worked swiftly. The burglar-proof section of her traveling bag opened in response to her ring-finger impress. Several medium-sized good-quality gems were extracted from its contents.

After much arguing and negotiating to establish a paper currency or credit system, gems still remained the interplanetary medium of private exchange. They were easy to carry, simple to evaluate in standard credits, impossible to counterfeit (at least it cost so much to make a gem that would pass spectrophotometric analysis that the real things were bargains by comparison), and, on all humanoid planets and most nonhumanoid ones, gems were highly desirable.

The outer section of the case provided Lahks with a gray-brown tunic, soft leather boots, and an over-the-shoulder pouch to replace the striking red-and-black traveling suit she had been wearing. Dressed, she looked in the mirror to check. A rather triangular face, framed in ash-brown hair cut straight across the forehead and square under the ears, stared back with tilted green-gray eyes. The eyes warmed, and the mouth, just a shade too large for the pointed chin, curved up. This was Lahks I, or Transform I; it was the way she remembered herself as a child before she learned she could look any way she wanted.

The major trouble with the Changeling property was the tendency to forget how you wanted to look. As a child, this had resulted in a constant shifting of color and feature. Lahks had to be confined with a "serious illness" for several months until she had learned the control principle. Unfortunately, there had never really been adequate opportunity to practice, and Lahks had compromised by working on five Transforms, which, once she thought of them, would lock in automatically until she consciously thought another Transform into being. Within each Transform she could make major or minor changes, or choose an entirely different appearance, but such effects had to be held with conscious effort. For short-term emergencies, total alterations were useful; for extended periods they were dangerous, owing to the tendency to slip back into one of the standard Transforms.

When Lahks was sure she was in and stable—Transform I was oldest and most familiar, but she had been using II for many years—she listened attentively at the door. The tiny pickup in her right earlobe informed her the corridor was empty. She slipped out, thumbed the lock-plate quickly, and in two jumps was halfway down the corridor. From there she could have come from any of several rooms and she walked sedately to the downwell and stepped on the plate. No eyes followed her as she walked quietly out of the hotel, an ordinary-looking girl in ordinary, inexpensive traveling clothes.

In the hotel the sunlight of late afternoon had filtered softly through windows that looked out on peaceful countryside. On the other side of the doorfield, cross streets offered psyche-shocking choices. Parallel with the main facade of the hotel, a wide, dignified thoroughfare showed elegant shops and cafes at mid-morning. At right angles, the screaming lights, sounds, and scents of a honky-tonk town on Saturday night presented a hurly-burly of wild entertainment, stalls filled with bizarre goods, and garishly lit Places of Pleasure.

Having glanced once at the night street, Lahks walked along the facade of the hotel and idled past the elegant shops, stopping now and again to examine a particularly appealing item. Halfway along she turned into a wide doorway completely surrounded by government seals. Here she exchanged her gems for GC notes that would be negotiable in Wumeera and made reservations for transport in the name of Tamar Shomra. The banker's clerk reached to turn off the privacy screen, but Lahks shook her head, leaned forward confidentially, and gave instructions. His face carefully blank, the clerk nodded and began to punch keys in the recorder beside him.

When Lahks emerged, her face wore a frown and her teeth held her underlip, as if she were deep in thought. She walked slowly back toward the hotel, her bulging pouch tightly clasped under her arm. When she was opposite the hotel entrance, she stood for a moment, as if irresolute; then with a furtive glance over her shoulder, she darted into the night alley. Before she had gone twenty meters, the bulging pouch was pulled sharply and its strap flapped loose. Lahks' green-gray eyes lit with anticipatory laughter showing tiny silver-gilt flecks. She had hoped someone from the Guild would have noticed her exit from the Bankers' Exchange and had made herself an ideal mark. There was little question that anyone attempting purse-snatching would be from the Guild. Local lightfingers were not encouraged at transshipment points. To survive in so small and easily policed an area, a thief or smuggler needed protection, and that was best afforded by the Guild.

Although the pull on her pouch had the true, sharp snap of the professional, Lahks' bag shifted only fractions of a centimeter. Simultaneous with the shifting came a low cry of alarm. Lahks turned on the instant, chuckling.

"Don't pull," she advised. "This is good stickfast. It will take the flesh off your bones before it lets go." Her voice was low, pleasant, carrying no threat. The smile that curved her lips was quite genuine.

The youngster who faced her sullenly, his hand invisibly welded to her pouch, was just what she had hoped for. Well dressed, well fed, looking like the scion of any well-off family, he was typical of a Guild man in a transshipment area. Within seconds of having her pouch, he would have deposited it at a convenient drop and blended into the crowd gathering around the victim.

"So I take a fall," he snarled. "Call Patrol and get me loose."

"No fall—not if you are as smart as I think you are," Lahks purred. "Just swing around, put your hand on my wrist, and we're two old friends taking a walk."

The suspicion in the boy's eyes was enormous, but he obeyed immediately. Every moment that he could delay being handed over to the Patrol was a moment more in which something might happen to free him altogether. So quick was the sequence of events, so low and brief the exchange of words, that any onlooker would think a young man had drawn a young woman's attention by touching her bag. Then they turned, greeted each other, and walked off together, the young man's arm protectively across the young woman's back. They did not hurry. Down the street was a Place of Pleasure. Lahks turned in at the door, her eyes more than ever alive with amusement.

Doubt, fear, and incredulity were so mixed in her captive's face that Lahks was tempted to ask for an amusement room just to see what he would do. It was, however, a very expensive joke, and there was the additional danger that the boy would be so frightened he would refuse to go. So young a male might prefer the tender mercies of the Patrol to those of a female who needed to trap her partner with stickfast. Lahks began to giggle. What an unholy mess it would make if the boy cried coercion and the case came to the Director's ears (all of them).

The Patrol was very strict about coercion even if they winked a little at Guild thieves. At transshipment points there could not, of course, be any rules about physical or sexual behavior. What was normal love-play for one race or culture might be the depths of degradation or even torture for another. This policy made transshipment stations a haven for "degenerates" of every culture. That harmed no one. Nine times out of ten any type of "degenerate" found willing partners. To prevent the tenth case from preying on the public, the laws of coercion had been promulgated. Stripped of their elaborate legal verbiage, these said that any act freely agreed upon by both parties, that did not culminate in death for either one, was legal; equally, any act, no matter how harmless physically, that was forced upon one party by another was illegal and punishable by law.

Actually, in spite of the knowledge that such an involvement would throw all her plans off schedule, Lahks would have yielded to the promptings of her worse self. Only the realization of the serious consequences to the boy she had caught restrained her. She wished him no harm at all. The fact that he was a thief was totally irrelevant to Lahks. A Guardian's morality was aroused by nothing less than a cosmic calamity. Thieves were part of the normal functioning of life, and no Guardian would interfere with one except for personal or tangential purposes.

Putting aside her vision of a really beautiful practical joke, Lahks requested a privacy booth from the attendant. A small quivering sigh by her side raised a whole new train of temptations, but Lahks ignored them firmly. Fun was fun, but if she wanted to do this business at all, she had better get on with it. Besides, the young man was so young—a lightfingers was very low on the Guild scale—that it was unfair to tease him.

When the soundproof panel closed behind them, Lahks said, "Strictly business. Let go of my wrist and I will let you loose. No fall for you and no embarrassing questions, so don't run. If you do, you will have to pay for the booth. First one out pays, you know."

"You sound as if *you* know," the boy snarled spitefully.

Indifferent to the jibe, Lahks slipped her free hand into the pocket of her tunic and brought out a flat spraytainer. With this she coated her pouch, arm, and the boy's hand. In seconds a faint warmth marked the chemical reaction that neutralized the stickfast. The boy backed away as soon as his hand came free, his sullen eyes on the pouch.

"I wouldn't," Lahks commented. "First of all, there is nothing worthwhile in it. The money was forwarded to my hotel. Secondly, I wouldn't want to hurt you, and I could. All I want is a recognition signal or a contact with the Guild. I have business on Wumeera. I might need help or transportation off-planet."

There was no change in the sullen expression, and Lahks was

21

annoyed. She understood why he was angry; she had trapped him and hurt his pride in his work. Also, he probably guessed she had been amused by his fear when she led him into the Place of Pleasure. But Lahks herself, whether caught in a harmless trap of her own or of someone else's devising, had far more tendency to laugh than to pout about it. The irritation passed as quickly as it came. Whether or not he gave her what she had asked for, her purpose was accomplished. He would report her to his superiors as someone overinterested in the doings of the Guild. They would watch her, and that in itself would be a lead to them.

Because Lahks preferred direct dealings in this case, however, she set herself to soothe the boy—she dared not use the drugs available to her because the Guild might detect them—and succeeded insofar as he finally told of a code to call, which, he said, could provide a contact for Wumeera. By now the timepiece on Lahks' wrist agreed with her inborn sense of time that about half a tu had passed. That was not ample, but it was adequate for two young people in a hurry. She suggested calmly that they leave.

Just beyond the door they parted. Lahks hurried now back to the day street and to a second hotel where the Bankers' Exchange had made a reservation and sent her money and a small selection of luggage purchased by an agent. It was a common-enough service. Many people changed identities at transshipment points. The second hotel was smaller, quieter, and rather more elegant than the first. By the time she reached it, Lahks was pleasantly aware that she had been picked up by a Watcher. Having registered, she chatted for a moment with the clerk, then asked him to send a meal to her room and then see that she was not disturbed. She did not space well, she admitted, with a tinge of embarrassed shyness, and was exhausted.

"Would you like the house physician to come up?" the clerk queried solicitously.

It was the last thing Lahks desired. She was efficient with external appearance, but her internal organs—either because Changelings were different, or because she did not pay strict attention to where the organs should be or what they should be doing—were often in a state that made physicians turn pale and check their psych condition. Since it never seemed to cause her any inconvenience, Lahks did not worry except when threatened by examination. She refused politely, saying all she needed was sleep.

The room was very handsome. Lahks smiled to herself as she stretched on the bed to rest and wait for her meal. Bankers' Exchange clients were always treated with respect. The fees they charged, Lahks decided, chuckling, deserved it.

"Dinner," the door said.

Lahks opened her eyes and pressed the release. The roboserv trundled in, opened itself, and presented a tasteful, well-arranged meal to which Lahks did complete justice. A touch on the "completed" button caused it to refold and trundle out with equal efficiency. Lahks did not watch it go, although she pressed the door release at the appropriate time. She rose, undressed, and put Transform I's clothes into the pouch, which she had turned inside-out. A cheap shift and alteration into Transform V turned her into a nondescript middle-aged woman who might easily be employed in some low capacity in such a place. By dropping her pulse rate to forty and lowering her body temperature to twenty degrees Centigrade, she convinced the Watcher that she was not herself (or was not there at all). Then it was quite safe to slip down the service stairs and out through the delivery entrance.

A secluded W.C. and a quick change back to Transform I permitted Lahks to walk into the first hotel with impunity. If anyone noticed, she was a guest who had gone out and was returning. Up to her room, shift back to Transform II, and stage one of phase two was successfully completed. Now she need only remove the essentials from the luggage that would go to Terra and carry on the normal activities of Transform II until "she" boarded ship. A reversal of the series of shifts of personality removed Lahks from the Terra-bound liner and brought her back to the second hotel in time for a late breakfast.

One thing Lahks noticed was that with each transformation she had an increasing desire to go on transforming, to giggle, to dance, to sing, to match her skin and hair color to the various wall surfaces and neon lights that flickered around her. It was a most interesting compulsion. Some day, she thought, when she had adequate supervision, she would have to yield to it and find out whether it would wear off naturally or become increasingly compulsive and dangerous. Perhaps Ghrey or Zuhema could have told her. With the thought came a cold wash of emptiness.

Lahks rose hurriedly and began to think hard about outfitting herself for Wumeera.

An open stall on the night street yielded spider-silk blankets and a sleeping bag, worn but serviceable. An expensive shop on the day street provided a stillsuit, the best available. A full tu was spent in fitting, 4 tu more in a hot-dry chamber. When Lahks emerged she was 0.572 kilos lighter. The stillsuit yielded 0.570 kilos of water. Another tu was devoted to finer fitting. The deserts of Wumeera are wide and hot; 0.002 kilos of water every 4 tu might easily be the difference between life and death.

Lahks also purchased a used stun-gun, a narcotic needler, and a laser. The weapons were primitive from a Guardian's point of view, but they might be useful and they were what a visitor to Wumeera would be expected to carry. The Watcher, which had been waiting faithfully at the second hotel, accompanied her throughout the several days she waited for the Wumeera transport. Only when she was on board and in her cabin did the small beep of its presence shut off. Lahks smiled and began to arrange her possessions commodiously. The continued interest of the Guild in her movements virtually guaranteed that the code frequency she had been given would summon a ship to Wumeera to take her off—if she could pay the price.

Chapter

3

Wumeera spaceport was something new in Lahks' experience. No guards or customs officials emerged to greet the ship. If that was a pleasant change, the fact that no robot cargo and baggage handlers were available was not. Lahks' luggage was unceremoniously dumped near some sheds at the periphery of the field, where it became her responsibility. The Free Traders were neither rude nor unkind; they were unable to help. As soon as the cargo they carried for Wumeera had been unloaded, they would space again. Although it was a regular stop, no man had ever been beyond the sheds where cargo was left.

"Where is the town?" Lahks asked.

"Somewhere there." The Cargomaster of the vessel gestured northwest over a sharp range of hills. "The spaceport was put in this cup because when the winds come they can topple a ship. I think the town is in another similar valley, but none of us has ever been tempted to look. What for? This is a world man made a mistake on. It should have been left alone to die. Are you sure you do not want to change your mind and go on with us?"

Lahks laughed. "No. I think I might like Wumeera if I ever get to see any more of it. But someone must come for the cargo. Will they take my luggage, too?"

"Likely. Likely they will. But this is a hard world. They might take it more thoroughly than you mean or want."

25

"If they will find a way to get my things into town, I will find a way to keep possession of them," Lahks said calmly.

The Cargomaster shrugged. A sense of mild obligation to a passenger and ordinary kindliness had impelled him to warn Lahks. He had done his duty. If she would not listen, on her head be it. Groundworms were altogether unaccountable creatures, anyway. He was relieved of further responsibility for this one by a straggling line of men and beasts appearing, as if by magic, out of a hillside not far away.

"Camels!" Lahks exclaimed with delighted disbelief. "No, there are two humps—dromedaries. I didn't know any survived, except in zoos. But here..."

"They are indigenous," the Cargomaster said, his normally austere face breaking into a broad grin. "They are the only good thing on this planet. Nice beasts, very nice. Unfortunately, the adults are too big to ship off-world, except as a curiosity, and no one has ever seen a young one. Apparently no one has any idea of how they breed, either."

By this time Lahks could see the creatures clearly and realized that, except for the size, the two humps on the back, and the spreading feet, they did not resemble dromedaries at all. They must be reptiles, she judged from the lizard-like face, the claws on the feet, and the scale-armor hide. But whoever heard of a reptile wearing bifocals and a silly smile? As the lead beast approached, it turned its head and observed Lahks and the Cargomaster, staring at them first from the upper lens and then from the lower lens of its large eyes. Then it stopped, sat down like a dog on its rear haunches, and grinned, if anything, more widely.

It was impossible to refrain from grinning back, and the beast bobbed its head as if in agreement, its eyes swinging dizzily from upper to lower lenses. Others came and sat alongside, also bobbing and grinning, and still others formed up behind. Lahks began to giggle. She sobered as the men who had accompanied the animals (for they certainly did not lead them) arrived and made their way through the squatting, bobbing pack. They were interesting, if not as charming as the beasts. They wore one-piece suits of something that looked disturbingly like the hide of their animals. Knee-boots of the same material shod them, and gloves, also of the same hide, were tucked into their belts. Each suit extended upward into a hood that was drawn down over the forehead and tight under the chin. Only the central portion of the face was exposed, and this was covered by a rigid, transparent shield clamped tightly at the temples and fitted under the chin so that it overlapped the hide suit. What Lahks could see of the faces was uniformly Mongolian in type.

The foremost of the men swung the shield up, and Lahks saw that it was hinged to the tight band that held it. "You have cargo for Landlord Vogil, Cargomaster? I am Hetman Vurn."

The galactic basic was as accentless as Lahks' own, but somewhat stilted, as if its pattern had been set at an earlier period and remained unchanged.

The Cargomaster nodded toward the shed. "It's all yours. No other shipment this trip. Do you want to check it?"

Hetman Vurn shook his head. "We have dealt with you often enough to know you, Cargomaster. If something lacks, we will report it on your next trip." He slapped his hip and the suit gaped open at the thigh, displaying a capacious pocket from which he extracted a sheaf of papers. "Further orders from Landlord Vogil and others."

He turned and pushed through the pack animals, which had stopped bobbing and merely squatted, grinning happily. When he reached one beast that Lahks had noticed was laden, he removed something from his pocket, slapped the pocket closed, and extended his hand toward the animal. A long, prehensile pink tongue emerged from the grinning mouth, delicately touched the Hetman's palm, and retreated between the quite respectable teeth. Hetman Vurn now returned to Lahks and the Cargomaster. The pack animal after twice trying to follow him directly finally backed out of the group and came around the side. Four men came forward and unloaded two small but heavy chests.

"As agreed, Cargomaster," Hetman Vurn said.

"Do you have ... anything else?"

The barely noticeable hesitation alerted Lahks. No one had mentioned heartstones on the Free Trader, and the ship seemed to make a perfectly adequate profit out of its regular delivery of goods; this oblique inquiry was the first indication Lahks had that there was off-world trade in heartstones.

"Not this trip, Cargomaster," the Hetman replied. He shrugged. "Next time, perhaps. There are always hunters. You have already loaded the goods from the shed?"

The Cargomaster nodded and Lahks was alerted again. She had not been asked to debark as soon as the ship made planetfall. She wondered whether it was to keep her from seeing the cargo. However, with his ship's business concluded, the Cargomaster was preparing to shed his final responsibility on Wumeera.

"This is Freelady Tamar Shomra. She has come to stay on Wumeera for private reasons. I hope your beasts can take her baggage into town?"

The Hetman looked curiously at Lahks. There were few types of business that could attract anyone to Wumeera. "Welcome to Wumeera, Beldame. There will be a drom to take your baggage. Would you like me to give a message concerning you to my Landlord? Perhaps he can help with your business."

"Perhaps he can," Lahks said with specious earnestness, but she was thinking of semantics. The Free Traders who dealt on many worlds used the form Freelady so that where slavery or serfdom was practiced there could be no doubt as to the status of their crew and passengers. On Wumeera, however, she was called Beldame; slavery was then unknown, but women were scarce or valuable or both, since all of them were called "beautiful lady." "I am looking," she said, giving no evidence that her mind was elsewhere, "for my brother, Absalom Shomra. He came here to find the jewel of the country, the one called the heartstone. We received two messages from him by private courier—and then nothing."

"He resembles you, Beldame?"

"Not at all," Lahks said. "He is very large—tall and strong. His face is broad, his hair very light, almost white; his eyes are a clear, pale blue."

The Hetman's eyes widened; then his face closed. Lahks' heart leaped into her mouth. Surely Hetman Vurn had recognized that description, and it was an accurate rendering of Ghrey's appearance. The void where Ghrey's signal had lived ached so that various rational explanations of Vurn's reaction were pushed aside in favor of the most unlikely. There had never been the smallest indication that Ghrey had touched on Wumeera, but, her heart cried, there was no evidence against it, either. Still, Lahks had enough control to ignore the Hetman's response; it was apparent that he had tried to conceal it.

"You must ask in the town," he said. "I live in the Landlord's manor and have little contact with strangers."

He turned away abruptly and shouted orders at his men for loading the cargo. Lahks watched his overabsorption in these details thinking that Hetman Vurn was a very bad actor. There could be no doubt at all that he knew something about a man who matched Lahks' description. She had no intention of pressing him just then. When she wanted, she would find out anything she desired to know. Meanwhile, she tried to close down the newly opened void. Her eyes rested absently on the men who were now loading until a peculiarity in the process drew her total attention.

As far as Lahks could see, the men neither led nor signaled to the animals in any way, yet one by one they rose and moved forward so that the trade goods could be loaded on them. Even more remarkable, it grew increasingly clear that it was the animal who decided how much of a load it would carry. When a large and obviously heavy crate was dragged out, Lahks saw something that woke her deepest instincts. Two of the animals looked at each other, rose together, and went forward. Even the need to find Ghrey momentarily slipped into second place. Those bifocaled, grinning, two-humped reptiles—if that was what they were—could be intelligent.

Before Ghrey, before the heartstone, before all else, this must be investigated. Nowhere in the records on Wumeera was a living, intelligent, indigenous species hinted at. Had intelligence developed in these most unlikely creatures, catalyzed by the presence of an imported thinking species? If so, it was Guardian business. Were minds trapped in a body that could give them no fulfillment? Lahks tried to remember whether such a case had ever been recorded and what, if anything, had been done about it. Her thoughts were interrupted by a soft nudge. She turned to find that one of the... people?... had inched up to her and was slyly prodding her with its snout.

Having drawn her attention, its head turned toward the baggage and it began head-bobbing again. Lahks picked up a bag and thrust it into a pannier. The head-bobbing increased in intensity, as if to show approval. Lahks was more certain than ever that some thinking process was taking place in that ridiculous head, but whether it was true intelligence or high-level instinct acted upon by long and frequent repetition needed to be determined, and this was not the time or the place. By the time Lahks was finished loading, the other droms had started off in the direction from which they had come. Lahks was now poked tenderly by the snout of the drom carrying her baggage so that she was prodded in the direction the others were moving. Lahks moved but looked back, as if for guidance. Carefully, as one would explain to a rather dull child, she was shown, without words, exactly where and how to go.

When they reached the spot from which the caravan had appeared so suddenly, Lahks saw that there was a narrow cut in the hill, a ravine-like cleft. It did not look like a natural feature to her, but she had no time to examine it because Hetman Vurn had dropped back and approached her.

"You have no windsuit?" he questioned and then answered himself, "No, they are not sold off-planet. Well, there is no wind today, praise Be. I see you have a heavy cloak. Put it on and cover your face completely when we come out of the cut. We must pass a flat—a small one, thanks Be. Your drom will guide you and shield you as much as possible. I do not think you will have trouble. If the wind should begin—which Be prevented crawl in between the forefeet of the drom. It will do its best to protect you."

Lahks cocked her head at the Hetman. "They are not animals, are they?" she asked. She was curious to hear what a Wumeerite would say—on many worlds enslavement of one intelligent species by another was cloaked by calling the enslaved animals. But Hetman Vurn said nothing; only shrugged his shoulders expressively.

"But you kill them for their skins to make the windsuits, don't you?"

Vurn burst out laughing. "Kill droms? How? Perhaps it might be possible by putting a fusion bomb down their throats. No one has tried that yet—I think. No, the windsuits are from a beast of another kind—a meeting with which Be prevented. Anything that lives here, except us, has the same kind of skin. Perhaps someday we will grow it, too."

Later, when they were safe in a second cut leading to the cup in which the town lay, Lahks reconsidered her decision to tear Hetman Vurn limb from limb. She realized he meant well by warning her, but his statement that there was no wind that day had been dangerously misleading. Now Lahks knew what "no wind" on a flat outside a cup meant. Her cloak was in shreds, a patch on one wrist was nearly skinned where it had been exposed for a few secs while she attempted to tighten a closure, and her whole body stung from the impact of particles through all the protective coverings. She had survived, she suspected, largely because the drom had shielded her from the full impact of a "calm day" on Wumeera.

Even if her rage against Vurn had not abated, she would have had no opportunity to vent it. The cut was narrow so that they traveled single file and, when they emerged near the town, her drom separated from the others and steered her firmly in another direction. Off to the right lay an ordered mass of low domed buildings surrounded by an odd-looking wall. To the left, in the direction she was being led, there was a much larger cluster of buildings. These were not walled, but except for that they were indistinguishable from each other and from the Landlord's property.

Free of the near presence of other humans, Lahks tried to "ask" the drom where it was taking her. Even without organs of speech a thinking being should be able to indicate a reply. The drom gave no indication of realizing it was being questioned, yet thought and decision had obviously taken place. The drom was taking her somewhere definite; it had recognized the fact that she did not belong with Hetman Vurn's group.

The "where" was soon answered. At a large dome, no higher than any of the others, merely of greater circumference, the drom stopped. The speaking tube was recessed into the building and was covered by a plate of the clear, vitreous substance the men had used as face shields. The door, peculiarly wide, fitted flush with the dome, its joint with the building covered by an overhanging flange. Lahks supposed the building to be the hotel, although there was no sign to announce it as such. She touched the clear cover and it popped off.

"Will you take a guest?" Lahks asked into the speaking tube.

With commendable promptness, the door opened. It neither swung nor slid, but pushed away at right angles from the building. As Lahks went in she saw the reason for its width. One could enter from either side, but the central portion was taken up by the huge mechanism that pushed the door outward. So much power to open a door?

A simian humanoid—one of those races that had developed intelligence late in its evolutionary process—regarded her questioningly. The threat inherent in the hulking four-hundred-kilo body, the beetling brows, the saber-like fangs, and long powerful arms was totally false. Like most races that had been dominant before developing intelligence, the gorls were very gentle. Since they had nothing to fear in their environment except natural catastrophes, their aggressive tendencies had been easily channeled by their intelligence into scientific achievement. By and large their worlds were paradises. In fact, it was very unusual to see a gorl off a gorl world.

"This is a hotel?" Lahks asked.

"More drinking house-meeting hall, but have beds."

The Basic sounded as if it were being produced by a boiling teakettle. Any species with vocal apparatus and a connected orifice with soft, flexible parts could speak Basic, but long, protruding fangs did not improve its clarity. The gorl language had never developed any sounds that necessitated closing the total orifice and humming behind it. Such sounds always hissed and bubbled in gorl Basic, although they remained recognizable.

"I'll take a bed. I expect to be here for a while. My baggage is outside."

The gorl gestured toward the interior of the dome. "Go through. Take any open room. Bring baggage from drom. Feed drom. Pay soon."

Lahks nodded and walked forward. The entire central section of the dome was obviously what the gorl had said, a drinking and meeting place. It was well lit by innumerable patches of the clear, vitreous stuff set throughout the ceiling. All around the circumference the walls merged into the upper portion of the dome and blocked off separate rooms. All the doors except three were open. A few showed fairly large rooms that contained tables and chairs—accommodations, Lahks assumed, for private parties and business meetings. The others were cubicles containing a bed, a chest, and an odd-looking chair. Lahks chose one that was as far as possible from any of the meeting rooms. Something told her that private parties on Wumeera were likely to be loud.

Within moments of making her choice, the gorl had followed with Lahks' bags. He put them down and held out a hand. "Five credits. Bed, food. Fed drom. Name Fanny."

Lahks opened her pouch and took out a twenty-GC note. The omission of all personal pronouns from gorl speech patterns sometimes caused difficulties in comprehension. Lahks grinned as she handed the note over. That dropping of personal pronouns had given and was giving the sem-psychs nervous breakdowns. Although the gorls had no words for "I," "you," "he," "she," or "it" in their own language and apparently could not bring themselves to say those words in any other language, they had a strong sense of individuality and personal possession. This, said the sem-psychs, was impossible. But, Lahks thought, so was traveling faster than the speed of light. You only had to find out how it was done to make it reasonable.

"Thank you, Fanny," she said. "My name is Tamar Shomra. Keep the whole note. I will be staying a few days, at least. Do you own this hotel?"

"Yes." The gorl nodded and bared his fangs in a ferocious snarl. Lahks remained unmoved, except to smile back at a polite gesture.

"It must be a great deal of work," she remarked.

"Not much. Barman serves drinks. Few come to Wumeera."

That was obviously a question as to Lahks' purpose although it was phrased as a statement. She had just opened her mouth to answer when a small voice at Fanny's belt said, "Door."

The gorl gestured around the room. "Need something, ask. Get comfortable. Come out. Have drink. Talk later." He then hurried away to work the mechanism that opened the door.

Lahks looked after him for a moment, then closed her own door. A few minutes later she came out with fresh clothing over her arm. A short survey showed her the fresher, fortunately close by. When she emerged the sudden dark of a desert climate had blacked out the transparent patches in the dome. Around the circular walls, smokeless torches burned, giving a dim, golden light. A few voices murmured in the central section where the round service counter was also torchlit. The barman moved softly, placing two mugs on the counter. A chair scraped as it was pushed back, the sound loud in the quiet room, and Lahks' eyes were drawn to the minor disturbance.

Chapter

4

Shock!

Joy! Emptiness filled!

"Ghrey!" Lahks cried, dropping her clothes and flinging herself across the room.

The broad shoulders of the man who had just risen twisted, and the blond head turned. Lahks, her arms outflung, skidded to a halt, gasped with terror, and then giggled weakly with relief. The blond giant with idiot's eyes turned fully and began to advance toward her.

"Shom, stop."

The giant hesitated, a look of indecision crumpling his face pathetically. Lahks dropped her arms and began to back away. The idiot's face twisted in pain and a silent wail of such misery and loss struck Lahks that she reeled.

"He won't hurt you. Don't be afraid of him."

There was panic in the voice that issued that assurance, but Lahks could not answer. First she had to deal with the hurt she had inadvertently inflicted. Words would not serve. Somewhere she had to find gladness. But that was beyond even her, just then. Ghrey had been given back to her and then snatched away again, all in a heartbeat. Yet it was not the fault of the now-cringing giant. Lahks pushed the little black button in her brain that turned her emotions off completely. A choked whimper came

34

from the idiot, a tiny sound, pathetic in its contrast with its maker's size.

There were arguments about whether or not telepaths could lie or be lied to; there were none about empaths. The creature Lahks faced now was surely empathic. He had reacted with warmth to her outpouring of joy and welcome, then with pain to her revulsion and rejection, and, worst of all, with terror to the cessation of emotional projection that must be the equivalent of death to an empath. Lahks took her finger off the black button in her brain. Warmth seeped back into her. Pity, kindliness, welcome to a fellow being, reassurance of acceptance.

"Come on, Shom, sit down."

A thin, brown hand, bone and whipcord, fastened on the giant's arm, but the idiot's eyes remained fixed on Lahks' face. She came forward and took his other arm.

"Yes, let's all sit down."

On such a planet there would be no privacy booths or screens for the tables. Fortunately, the place was not crowded. Perhaps it was too early, or perhaps it was never crowded. All three sat at a round table about halfway back from the service counter. Automatically, Lahks patted the idiot's hand, but now her eyes sought the other man.

Her immediate impression was of a feral being—a sly running animal, lean and lithe, hunted and hunting. Fear and shock showed in the eyes that were lit by a remnant of red hate that was rapidly fading into a cautious acceptance. The man himself was a Terra-type humanoid, dark and sleek of skin, eyes, and hair. The lips were thin, the nose sharp and a trifle hooked; an expression of intense alertness added to the weasel-like impression. Both men were dressed in worn, common coveralls. They did not look like natives, nor as if they were prosperous. A plan, full and complete, leaped into Lahks' mind.

"I'm sorry I startled your . . . friend?"

"I'm sorry he startled you." Without its overtones of panic, the dark man's voice was a light, pleasant tenor. The flatness of the statement, however, gave no implied answer to Lahks' question.

"I thought he was someone I . . . I knew. From the back . . ."

"Yes, he's a perfect Shomir type. I guess they do look a lot alike from the back." He smiled, white teeth gleaming through thin, dark lips, the canines a little longer, a little sharper-pointed

35

than normal. "You were kindness itself to sit down with us. Fanny said if Shom scared someone else we would have to leave. Where the hell else is there to go on this planet?"

"I don't know. I have only just arrived myself. My name is Tamar Shomra."

"Tamar of Shomir? You are no Shomir."

Lahks shrugged. "Half. My father was in Trade."

"The Shomir do not trade." Suspicion sharpened his voice, but he shook his head. "None of my business. Sorry."

"Perhaps it is your business, or will be." Lahks gestured with her head. "Is he always so hard to handle?"

Heat flickered in the dark eyes. "Not unless someone gets to him. Are you a telepath or an empath?"

Lahks widened her eyes. "Not a receiver, but it is not impossible that I am a weak sender. Many Shomir are one or the other. My mother was a Shomir. You are perfectly right. The Shomir do not go into Trade. I was... well... overcome by emotion. I had better tell you."

No change of expression, no quiver of muscular contraction indicated the suspicion that must be aroused by her ingenuousness. Lahks was well satisfied. That the dark man should watch her and be suspicious could do no harm. Although the story she was about to tell would be a tissue of lies, it would grow more and more truthful in appearance because the purposes she claimed were true. These men were almost certainly for hire—one way or another—and they seemed ideal. Lahks felt a lifting of spirits, a welling of ever-ready laughter. She was traveling a rainbow of good fortune and the pot of gold at the end of it would be Ghrey.

The big hand she was patting moved. Lahks turned. Shom was smiling. Lahks caught her breath, smiled back, then touched his face with her fingers.

"He wasn't always this way. What happened to him?" she asked.

The lean shoulders lifted, showing knobs of bone under the thin coveralls. Lahks wondered briefly if the dark man ate enough or if he was older than he looked. Certainly Shom gave no sign of undernourishment. The loyalty factor seemed enormous, and since Shom would be no trouble this could be molded into quite a team.

"What happened? His mind-partner died, very horribly,

36

while they were linked. That is the fact. Beyond that is all
guesswork. There is a lot the med-psychs do not know. They
think Shom—that is not his name, but he answers to it—stayed
linked to . . . to give comfort. He was a physical mess when it was
over. It was a miracle the stigmata did not kill him. As for his
mind—who knows? Burned out, it may be, or in such deep-
shock retreat that nothing could reach it."

Inside Lahks' breast, emotion twisted painfully. Shom
uttered a small whimper and reached toward her. She slid her
arm across his hulking shoulders, hugged them briefly, then
patted his back.

"Not to worry, Shom," she soothed. "It's all right. Not to
worry." Reassurance flowed from her. The big man, childlike in
his immediate response, smiled again. Lahks nodded, returned
her attention to the dark partner. After looking at him for a
moment, she drew a datarec from her belt and laid it on the
table, but without pushing the start switch. "Yes," she said, "I
will tell you. I think I can offer you a Deal that will benefit us all,
but I need to know a few things first."

"Deal first, then information."

Lahks frowned. She did not want to seem too eager. "So you
can fit the information to the Deal?" Then, without waiting for
the answer, she laughed. "Why not? As long as the story can be
fixed to explain what I want explained, why should I care?"

"I don't want trouble with the Guild."

Lahks shuddered. "I hope not. We might need them to get us
out of here." She grinned. "No cautions about the Patrol?"

"You said you had Trade connections. The Patrol will always
listen to Trade."

Laughing, Lahks replied, "So will the Guild." Then she
sobered, pushed the start on the datarec, and put her left hand
on the table, palm up.

"Deal Name: Tamar Shomra."

It did not matter what name she gave. As soon as it was
started, the datarec identified the individuals involved in any
business or personal contract. It made visual, aural, and bio-
physchem records that could not be altered or erased. Although
the machine could be destroyed, the molecular records were easy
to reconstruct. There were ways to get around a datarec. There
were ways to get around anything, but for ordinary people and
even ordinary criminals, the record of a datarec was the ultimate

guarantee. Lahks wanted to be taken seriously; once she switched on the datarec, there could be no doubt of her intentions.

The dark man put his hand on the table, too, palm down, but he did not touch hers. He was willing to listen, but not to commit himself.

"Deal Name: Wesel Stoat."

Lahks allowed herself a little chuckle. The name was undoubtedly as fictitious as her own, but the choice showed a sense of humor to which her whole being responded. Imagine a man who looked like that calling himself weasel-weasel! Lahks did not allow her appreciation to divert her from the business at hand.

"Deal Merchandise: Heartstones." She saw the muscles in Stoat's hand quiver, but it was impossible to judge whether the instinct had been to withdraw or to make contact.

"Deal Question: Personal or commercial?"

"Deal Answer: Both." Lahks closed her hand but did not remove it from the table. Stoat's hand closed also without withdrawing. He was prepared to listen to her explanation and recognize it was not part of the Deal. "I told you my father was in Trade. He has had misfortunes of various kinds. He was finally driven to make Contract for a heartstone."

"Then he has just added a final calamity to his misfortunes."

"There are heartstones. I have seen dead ones and read everything about them."

"There are heartstones, but you do not pick them up in the public street."

"I know that, but this is important, not just commercial. You saw how I reacted to Shom. I have a brother—half brother—Absalom, my mother's son out of her first husband. Even so, we were close and my father was crazy about Ab. He wasn't a good Trader; he had too many religious convictions. But he was an incipient empath and marvelous as a first-contact man and Deal Reader. Well, about five S-years ago he disappeared on a first contact. My father was wild. We did"—Lahks shook her head—"everything."

"I can see why you were startled by Shom."

Lahks nodded acceptance, but she did not divert from her story. "There was no trace... none. One day he was there, the next day he was gone. Nothing else was missing or disturbed—

tent, bedroll, supplies and there was no evidence of antagonism among the locals. One of them, a hunter who had been out at night, said he had seen a new light in the sky."

Shom stirred uneasily in his seat, reacting to the genuine distress Lahks felt as she described her father's disappearance. Stoat's eyes flickered to the big man and the cynicism faded a little in his eyes. He lifted his hand from the table. Lahks stopped speaking at once.

"Shom, go get us some drinks."

The idiot rose at once. Lahks also lifted her hand from the table. What she was about to say had no connection at all with the Deal. "How much of what we say does he understand?"

"I have no idea. He follows direct instructions quite intelligently, even pretty complicated instructions when they relate to physical acts. On the other hand, any abstract question even what his name is or how he feels if he does not have an immediate physical sensation to describe gets no response."

"Does he talk?"

For a reply Stoat gestured toward the service counter. Shom was just rumbling "Three drinks" in a bass voice.

"He talks enough to get what he needs, but he never *says* anything—if you know what I mean."

Lahks nodded, then lowered her clenched hand to the table again. Stoat responded with a similar action. "I won't upset him again, I hope. Just raking up Ab's disappearance..." Her voice faltered. She set her lips, paused, then went on steadily. "After a long time my father was ready to give up. He left feelers out, of course, but he thought Ab was dead. Only my mother said he wasn't. She is not a telepath and not even as good a Deal Reader as Ab, but she insisted Ab was alive somewhere out there." Lahks gestured in the direction she remembered as that of Ghrey's sending. "So we kept looking, but 'there' covers a lot of space."

Shom returned with the three stone mugs clasped in one hand. He set them down, passed them around. Lahks drank thirstily, damping down reawakened sorrow and new enthusiasm.

"We finally got a message—a real weirdie. It was from Necrocivita." Stoat's hand quivered, almost lifted. Lahks hesitated until it was set steadily on the table again. "All it said

39

was that if a heartstone was delivered, Ab would turn up and my
father's misfortunes would be canceled. Well, we ... uh ... tried
other things, but in the end my father made Contract."

"And sent you alone?"

Lahks opened her hand. No outside help, except what they
could get for themselves, was part of the Deal. "Deal Answer:
Alone. I told you my father had misfortunes. He was not free to
come."

Stoat's eyes narrowed. A "not free" Trader meant total
financial disaster—a ship sold or impounded at worst, lack of
sufficient money for liftoff fuel and supplies at best (which only
led to the worst in a short time). He opened his hand.

"Deal Question: If the Trader is not free, where will we find a
profit? Deal Corollary: Necrocivita does not pay in gems, and I
have no interest in their form of payment."

"Deal Answer: What will not suffice for a Trader is often
enough for a party. Deal Question: Do you want to discuss
terms?"

There was a long pause. Finally Stoat closed his hand. He
was drawn to this young woman in a way that made him very
wary, but his situation demanded that he place physical survival
before emotional problems. "I thought you wanted to ask
questions."

"You have already answered many of them. They were
mostly about Shom. The others concern the details of the story
for the locals. Somehow I have the feeling that an eye is kept on
heartstone hunters and that not many reap the profits of their
labors."

Stoat laughed shortly and bitterly. "You are not as innocent
as you look."

Lahks laughed, too. "I am a Trader's daughter."

He nodded, opened his hand suddenly, and laid the palm
against hers.

"Deal Question: Final or open-end?" he asked.

"Deal Answer: Open-end."

"Deal Question: Whose option?"

"Deal Answer: Mutual."

"Deal Statement: Open-end terms on mutual agreement
accepted."

The palm-to-palm contact was changed into a brief grasp.
Stoat broke the hand clasp, closed his fist, and lifted his mug.

"Nice feel to your hand, Trader's daughter. There might be a Contract in this."

She waited until he had drunk and reestablished contact.

"Deal Offer: First-part terms contingent on completion of Deal. One-half value of take, paid in gems, GC notes, or kind. Referee valuation acceptable."

Suspicion flared suddenly in Stoat's eyes. The terms were far too generous. Lahks did not care. Let him watch, spy, suspect. Since she had no intentions of cheating him, his suspicions could only end in confirming his confidence in her. She was only interested now in making Contract and working out the details of the hunt.

"Deal Question," Stoat snapped. "What payment can be in kind when merchandise is one heartstone?"

"Deal Answer: We could seek two heartstones. Other contingent merchandise noted on this planet."

"Deal Question: State other contingent merchandise."

"Deal Answer: The skins of which windsuits are made. The clear, vitreous substance used for face plates and lights. A live drom, if they can live off-planet."

"Deal Statement: Contingent merchandise accepted." Once again Stoat broke contact and closed his hand. "It is accepted, Trader's daughter, but you do not know what you are saying." Even as he shook his head, however, his eyes brightened and his lips twitched. "If we could get off-planet with such a load ... By the Power that Is, your father's misfortunes *might* be canceled." He burst into laughter. "Maybe those spooks at Necrocivita do know what they're talking about. But you better have contact with Trade and with the Guild—and perhaps with the Power that Is, too."

Over her own closed fist, Lahks said, "You will have to brief me on the difficulties of getting out, but let us try to make Contract first." She opened her hand. Stoat's came to meet it immediately. She asked at once, "Deal Question: First-part terms acceptable?"

"Deal Statement: First-part terms, contingent on completion of Deal. One-half value of take paid in gems, GC credits, or kind, including contingent merchandise, referee valuation acceptable. First-part terms accepted."

The brief handclasp that signaled acceptance physically was repeated and Lahks began again immediately.

"Deal Offer: Second-part terms. No contingency beyond effort in Deal. Off-planet transport if desired only."

"Deal Question: Regarding second-part terms. Payment for time? Who bears hunt expenses?"

Lahks frowned. "Deal Statement: No payment for time. Individual costs of hunt to be borne by each individual."

"Deal Offer: Second-part terms rejected."

Stoat's voice was sharp, even tinged with a little anger, but relief showed in his eyes. Lahks pursed her lips as if she was considering a new offer. This haggling was childish, but it was necessary to act in character with her part as a Trader. The Deal was so chancy and the take—if they made it—would be so high that it was good Trading to offer a high cut, but to insist on the others paying their own expenses and working free. If they failed to make a take, the whole Deal would cost her nothing but her own living expenses. She laughed aloud, slipped her hand from under Stoat's, and closed it.

"So I did not catch you. Are you sure there is no Trade in your blood?"

"The only thing I am sure is not in my ancestry is a methane-breathing ice wriggler," Stoat replied. But almost before the words were out his hand was flat, raised invitingly just enough for Lahks to slip her palm under.

Now it was Lahks who hesitated. She could not let him push her too far. If they got the heartstone, there would be no problem. Either it would help her find Ghrey, in which case the Guardians would pay Stoat's claims, or it would not help her, in which case they could sell it and she could pay off that way. At present her funds, although substantial, were limited. Slowly she slid her hand forward.

"Deal Question: Make counter-offer."

"Deal Offer: No contingency beyond effort in Deal. Standard day payment, five GC per man. Tamar Shomra pays all costs of hunt. Transport off-planet paid by mutual consent at termination of Deal."

"Deal Offer: Rejected," Lahks snapped. She closed her hand. "If I wanted those terms, I could have brought my own crew."

"And they would have been about as much help on Wumeera as a Skingol amphibian. I know this planet. I have been out there." His head jerked toward the western desert. "I even know how to get your contingent merchandise. I am offering you experienced men—and don't worry, Shom pulls his weight and more on the cheap."

Lahks shook her head. "Maybe so, but the only way I could test that would be to offer someone else a Deal. And you must realize my resources, especially while on this planet, are limited." She reached toward the "off" button on the datarec. Stoat grabbed her hand.

"I'm in a hole, too," he confessed. "I would like to come to Contract, but I can't afford to be dumped off-planet, and possibly be left at a transfer point, flat broke. How about if you pay expenses and a flat fee?"

"Expenses might run pretty high on Wumeera," Lahks protested. "I don't even have a windsuit."

Stoat sucked air through his teeth, let his eyes run over Lahks, and smiled suddenly. "Usually they do because the bearer buys all new equipment, but they won't run high this time. Shom and I have complete hunting gear." Quite suddenly, the smile still on his lips, his eyes went hot and angry. "They never take that. They want you to go out again and again and again. I swore I wouldn't, not if I starved first, but *you* have Trade connections. By the Power, how I would like to do them!" He paused, taking a deep breath. "I suppose I shouldn't have said that, but it doesn't matter. I have sixty-two GC and that." He dropped a handful of local coin on the table. "Even if I wanted to, I could not share expenses. Offer me a Contract, any Contract I can take, and I will take it."

Chapter

5

Once Contract was made, Stoat relaxed as far as his quivering alertness was capable. He sent Shom for more drinks, grinned his sharp-toothed grin, and shook his head.

"Trader's daughter, I had to take you for a fee. Years ago people got away with heartstones, but that was years ago. The Landlords are organized now. You find the stuff; they find you and take it away."

"It is a big planet," Lahks replied calmly. "The first thing to do is to get lost on it."

A startled glance in Stoat's dark eyes melted almost immediately into comprehension. Since it was obvious that hunters were watched by various methods, it was best to have a logical reason for leaving town unconnected with heartstones or other merchandise. Circumstances were in their favor, Lahks pointed out as soon as she discovered that Stoat and Shom had come in from the desert rather than on a ship. This would fit very well with the story she had told Vurn—which was true, except that Ab had not disappeared from Wumeera. All Lahks needed to do was "recognize" Shom as her brother.

"His mental condition would make it imperative to a fond sister to get him off-planet and into psych care as soon as possible," Lahks said cheerfully, drinking large gulps of the sour green wine in the mug. She pursed her lips. "Can I get a windsuit early tomorrow, Stoat?"

"Probably. You are small." His eyes assessed her chest development. "A boy's castoff will probably fit."

"Good. That first. Then how do I get to see the Landlord?"

"Walk up to the manor and ask. They might turn me away. You, he'll see." Stoat grinned wolfishly, then said, "I wouldn't. Wumeera's a hard planet and women are... valuable property. You would get in, but you might not get out."

"The Cargomaster said the locals might steal my luggage, and they did not even look at it. Is this more of the same?"

"Evil-minded suspicion? Perhaps. I have never known of a case firsthand," Stoat chuckled. "Well, it is not likely that anyone would try to abduct me for my feminine charms. I have heard rumors—that's all. I had better go with you."

"Don't be a fool," Lahks said sharply. "Even if they let you in, would the Landlord remain unguarded in your presence or let you carry arms in? If he wanted to keep me, you would present no difficulties. I have been in Trade all my life. Do you think this is the first Deal I have worked alone? I can take care of myself."

The next day Stoat, Shom, and Lahks went shopping. Stoat had told Shom to stay behind, and Lahks reinforced the command mentally, but the big man's face mirrored such misery and his mind wailed its loss so pathetically that the decision was immediately reversed.

"It's better to take him, anyway," Lahks rationalized. "A fond sister would not leave her defenseless brother alone. If I pet him in public, word will get back to the Landlord. Every bit of evidence helps."

Stoat led them slowly down along the alley between the featureless domes. He chose one that, although smaller than Fanny's hotel, seemed to Lahks indistinguishable from all the others. When the door opened to his shout, however, it was into the shop of a dealer in local products. Lahks framed an ingenuously admiring question as to how, if he had not been in the town for long and had his own equipment, he knew exactly the place he wanted.

"Speaker tube," he replied absently, not sensing her suspicion. "Color-coded and shaped. Hotel shows red and has a mug shape. Shops show money sign. Green for local stuff, yellow for imports, or any combination when they handle both. Exchanges use diamond shapes striped in gold and silver. Private domes are round and usually leave the tube material undyed. Here." He lifted a shimmering windsuit from a counter. "Try this."

Lahks was astounded at the suppleness of the garment. She found the flexibility was the result of thousands of tiny interlocking and overlying scales attached at a single pivot point to the hide beneath. That, too, was unlike any animal skin she had ever seen. It was black and slick and, according to Stoat, a perfect insulator. Boots and gloves were also readily obtained, but the face mask presented unexpected problems. Finally, after much rooting around, a mask of the proper curvature and a sufficiently narrow headband were found.

Lahks bought the equipment, accompanying the purchase with naïve remarks about how interested her friends and family would be in the remarkable material. She appealed repeatedly to Shom in the most tender terms to agree with her, to tell her how she looked. And, upon receiving no reply other than his aimless smile, she protested heatedly to Stoat that he did recognize her, he did.

"It may be, Beldame," Stoat replied with his sinuous shrug. "But whether he does or not, the quicker you get him off-planet and into the hands of competent psych men, the better it will be."

This seed planted and immediate needs cared for, they returned to Fanny's, where the midday meal was making the air pleasantly redolent. This, like supper the night before, was a stew consisting of round sections of a spongy, but tender, meat, cubes of some fungus-type plant, things that looked like bean sprouts and bamboo shoots, and a variety of more familiar Old Terra-type vegetables.

There were a fair number of local residents present. Lahks confined her attention to Shom, petting him, urging him to eat, and speaking to Stoat only of the possibility of obtaining early passage off-planet. To the latter remarks Stoat replied that ships were not frequent, but the Landlord would know when another was due. Lahks stopped Fanny as he went by.

"Can I get someone to take me to the Landlord's manor?" she asked the gorl.

Fanny glanced at Stoat and then drew his lips back from his fangs. "Mad at Landlord, eh?" he remarked to Stoat. "No good.

No help." He turned his attention to Lahks. "No need. Drom come. Drom lead." He watched Lahks for a moment, the bright intelligence of his eyes strangely at war with his simplistic speech. "Find seek?" he asked, but the question was rhetorical, because he nodded at Shom. "Good take away. Bad here. Frighten people. No harm but makes afraid."

Lahks smiled tremulously. "My brother. It is a miracle that he should be here, where I landed. I thought I would have to search and search. I am sure our psych men can cure him. See how he smiles at me? I know he recognizes me."

Shaking his head, Fanny half-turned away, then swung back to bend low, his eyes on Stoat. "Don't say go. Landlord never let hunter go. Not five, eight orbits. Hunter not go, hunter not tell what Landlord take." He drew back and said in a more normal voice, "Maybe not stone-sick. Maybe see big sand crab or big silverfish. Get shocked. Then psych men make better."

"Stone-sick?" Lahks questioned.

"Some touch stone, everything goes away." An expression flickered across the anthropoid face and Lahks, who knew how hard it was for nonsimians to see their changes of expression, realized that some really powerful emotion was shaking the gorl. "Once had stone," Fanny added. "Gone now. Stolen. Get another someday. Wait. Never go home without stone."

Lahks felt chilled and shuddered openly. "Dreadful things!" she cried. "I wouldn't take one for a gift! I wouldn't touch one for anything! Look what it did to my brother. I must get him home quickly."

A quick flicker of admiration warmed Stoat's eyes, but he kept them lowered. He appreciated her consummate acting, although he did not intend that anyone else should. Nonetheless, he did not want any suspicion of a hidden heartstone to cling to them. "I don't think he is stone-sick," he said softly, but clearly enough for his voice to carry to those who might be listening. "Certainly he did not have one on him when I found him. His camp was intact. No sign of a fight or robbery. There were other bed packs, though. Looked to me as if his guides had gotten caught by a land crab or a silverfish. If they had gotten a stone and run off with it, they would have taken their packs. If you take him home, out of these surroundings, perhaps he will recover."

Later in the afternoon, when rumor had time to drift up to

the manor, if it was going to drift, Lahks came out alone. She had not walked ten steps, thinking largely of the satisfactory comfort of her stillsuit topped by the windsuit and face mask, when a drom sidled up to her. It grinned, bobbed, and suddenly collapsed right in her path, its forelegs, incredibly, folding forward as if its knees were hinged backward. Lahks giggled as she accepted the invitation and seated herself between the humps.

She had expected to feel a knobby spine, as one did whenever an animal was ridden bareback. Instead she sank into a flat, soft, and resilient surface, much like a spaceship foam chair. Looking down to check sense against vision, Lahks observed a flat ridge about eighteen centimeters wide rippling up the drom's abdomen. It was something she had never noticed before. It was, frankly, an unnatural structure in appearance. Lahks could not imagine a purpose for it, either, until, seconds later, the ridge rose, touched her feet, rose another two centimeters, and stiffened to provide a solid, comfortable footrest.

The drom got up so smoothly that Lahks hardly noticed the change in position and started off toward the manor. Lahks' head whirled. She leaned forward, her ear against the drom's side below the hump. Truly she expected to hear the whirr of gears, the high whine of some cybernetic comic's idea of the perfect, useful joke. All that came was the slow susurrus of unlabored breathing, the regular thump of a strong heart, and the occasional slight gurgle of a digestive system.

It was impossible! What living creature could change its form in seconds to suit its purpose? The question had barely articulated in her brain when the answer came—I can, a little. A Changeling? The drom? With all the force she could muster, Lahks thrust silent questions. Who are you? What are you? In a moment she desisted. The droms were not a newly discovered phenomenon. Doubtless better minds than hers had worked at them. But of all the myriad creatures of the universe, intelligent and nonintelligent, only single-celled amoeboids and the Changelings could significantly alter their form.

In a very large universe, coincidences were neither impossible nor even infrequent. In fact, totally disparate lines of evolution had produced species so similar genetically that they were capable of interbreeding. Still, there was something about the droms, something familiar. Not familiar in the sense that they reminded Lahks of something she knew or remembered familiar in a more basic way, as the hysterical gaiety caused by many rapid transformations had been familiar. A genetic memory? A dim consciousness of racial experience? Impossible to pin down without long, deep analysis, but there was some connection between the tickling hilarity of rapid transformation and the lovable ludicrousness of the droms.

The train of thought was interrupted by the smooth-flowing crouch of the drom. An open gate in the manor wall was to Lahks' immediate left. She slipped from her seat, patted her mount affectionately, and turned toward the gate. The drom rose and ambled off. As Lahks walked in, a guard straightened up from his lounging position.

"You desire?" he asked pleasantly.

"Hetman Vurn," Lahks began hesitantly.

"A moment and he will be summoned."

"It may not be needful," Lahks replied, insensibly slipping into the slightly archaic speech pattern of the native and deliberately sounding unsure. "Hetman Vurn said he would mention me to the Landlord. He thought..."

"A moment, Beldame," the guard repeated, then signaled to another man farther back.

The title of respect indicated that news of Lahks was already widespread in the manor. It was, in fact, only a few moments before Vurn appeared, dressed in a well-cut tunic and breeches. Lahks pushed her face mask higher up.

"I found my brother," she said in a tight voice.

The Hetman nodded sadly. "I was afraid it would be so, but I did not wish to be the bearer of bad tidings. It *might* have been a coincidence."

"At least I found him and he is alive." Lahks smiled a sad little half-smile. "I feared worse. We have men who cure sick minds on my home but the longer the sickness, the harder the cure. I must take my brother home, Hetman, as quickly as possible."

"You had better speak to the Landlord, Beldame."

Vurn led Lahks past two small domes that were probably guardhouses, around another, larger one, the purpose of which she could not guess, to a third that was larger than Fanny's hotel.

This had a row of the vitreous plates across the door and well around the sides at about eye level for a man. The Hetman made a series of musical sounds, perhaps words in an ancient, long-dead Mongolian tongue, into the speaker tube. Lahks automatically committed sound and tone to memory. The door opened into a wide corridor flanked by many closed doors. Vurn spoke briefly to the guard who had admitted them, then opened the nearest, right-hand side door, which slid silently into the wall on noiseless tracks.

"If you will wait here, Beldame, the Landlord will see you in a few minutes."

It was a well-furnished reception room, lit by the ever-present transparent panels in the wall and softly glowing light plates in the ceiling. The floor was covered by a magnificent carpet, the fabric of the easy-rest chairs rippled in myriad soothing colors. Small tables, tastefully placed, invited the setting down of food and drink.

Vurn stood aside politely for Lahks to enter. In the doorway she paused, reached into her belt pouch with one hand, and pointed to a nearby table with the other.

"How lovely. Of what is that made?"

Vurn looked, then turned to Lahks courteously. She was just placing a smoke stick between her lips. "Native stone, Beldame. The designs are carved by the wind." He laughed. "Even the wind has its uses. You would care to eat? To drink?"

"I have eaten, but a cool drink would not come amiss."

Vurn bowed Lahks to a chair, the nearest to the door, and stepped out. Smoothly, and too swiftly for Lahks to have caught it even from the position she had chosen, the door slid shut. Lahks listened intently; the latch did not click. Swift and silent, she was at the door. A fingertip, an infinitesimal movement, proved it to be free. The tiny device she had touched to its lip had, indeed, prevented the latch from catching. She did not know, of course, whether the door would have locked upon closing, but safe was better than sorry.

The precaution seemed unnecessary. In a few minutes Vurn was back with an invitation to the Landlord's presence. He had taken the liberty, he said politely, of bringing her drink to the audience chamber. If she did not wish to ingest in public, a privacy screen could be arranged. Lahks disclaimed any eating or drinking taboos and followed him readily, so close at his heels that she had to step sideways near the door. The motion of the fingertip that removed her device was infinitesimal. The gesture that replanted it on the door of the audience chamber was equally unnoticeable.

Landlord Vogil was an older, stockier version of Vurn, magnified by an aura of authority. Only an enormous amount of interbreeding, Lahks thought as she repeated the tale of the loss of her brother and described finding him in Fanny's hotel, could account for the great similarity of appearance of these people. Stoat was more likely to be right about the need for off-planet women than the Cargomaster was about the baggage. There was plenty of evidence of imported luxuries, but Lahks had not seen a single woman since she had arrived. Women were therefore terribly scarce or kept in purdah.

The expression in the Landlord's eyes was enough to bring certainty on that score. Yet Vurn had only seemed mildly admiring, not hungry. Lahks lowered modest eyes to keep the amusement at her own stupidity hidden. Vurn knew she was Landlord's meat as inaccessible as the stars. In so rigidly structured a society, it would take great, perhaps suicidal, daring to covet Landord's meat.

For a moment Lahks allowed herself the luxury of imagining her capture and the Landlord's subsequent fate. This so tickled her fancy that giggles rose in her throat, making her voice quiver and tears mist her eyes. Seldom had a sister seemed more emotionally involved with her brother's disaster. Still, it was no part of Lahks' mission to drive a Landlord mad and disrupt a whole community. Wumeera had enough troubles without Guardian interference. Surreptitiously, she began to massage the ball of her fourth finger with her thumb. From its flesh-colored sheath implanted under her nail, a tiny transparent needle slid forward and locked into place. It would be enough, if necessary, to convince the Landlord that she was repellent and had better be sent away.

"The longer the damage remains," she concluded, "the harder it is for the surgichems or the psychs to repair. Can you help me get a ship? You have a Carroll radio, don't you? Could you call a ship?"

The Landlord shook his head. "I have the radio, and I would

be glad to oblige you, but it would be no good."

Had she misjudged the situation, Lahks wondered as she protested in a trembling voice, "But surely a ship would answer an emergency call. I would be willing to pay passage plus the off-course penalty."

The Landlord should have said he would call, should have offered to send for her brother, offered the hospitality of his house. Once the fly was in his web, he could do as he liked—but he was shaking his head again.

"We have no port. Only ships with self-landing, self-lifting craft could stop. That would be Patrol or Free Trade. The chance of Patrol being in the area is very small indeed. This is a peaceful stable planet." He laughed softly. "The next Free Trade ship due to set down here will be half a year from now."

"You mean no ship will come to this planet at all for half a year?" Lahks' voice rose with fearful incredulity.

"No, no, Beldame. I mean at this cup. A ship is due a month or three weeks from now at Landlord Tanguli's cup."

"You could call, tell the ship to make another landing here, couldn't you?"

"I could. I doubt the Free Trader would do it. The fuel expenditure is so great. Doubtless it would mean he would be forced to forgo another stop. I doubt you could recompense him for the loss. Sometimes there are even delivery penalties."

"But what am I to do?"

"It is not so far to Landlord Tanguli's cup, although one must cross a desert flat and a range of hills. With a guide... I would call Tanguli and tell him you were coming so that he could inform the Cargomaster that there would be passengers."

He went on to describe the needs of such a journey, but Lahks was seeing and thinking about the plan he was truly formulating. Stoat and Fanny had mentioned the new cooperation among the Landlords. Probably if Vogil tried to keep her now, there would be an accounting of some kind with his peers. If she set out across the desert and was "lost," Vogil could easily disclaim responsibility. Once she was immured in his inner rooms, who was to say she had been abducted rather than having died in the lonely wastes?

Flexing her hands in a nervous gesture, Lahks sighed, "I don't know. I don't know. I must get him home, and yet the danger would be so great. I must think it over."

"As you will, Beldame," Landlord Vogil replied patiently. "I can furnish you with a guide, but there are plenty of men in the town who would go. It is not a particularly dangerous trek. It is done often."

Chapter

6

Stoat was not happy. His eyes flickered restlessly and his lips were thinned so that his long canines peeped through. They were safe enough for the moment in Stoat's stilltent, crammed into a shallow scrape of a cave. It would only be hours, he suspected, before the hunt started. His sidelong glance slid over Shom to the sleeping girl.

Hunter and hunted, Stoat had developed the fatalism of an animal. He knew by some inner instinct when he would be successful and when he would fail. Neither mattered much; the hunt was all, because in the end there was only the final failure, which was the final victory. He was of the old one-God faith, His Power, the unnameable Yahweh, was immutable Justice weaving through irrational paths, and Its sign was the six-pointed star.

But the girl had upset his balance. He could not read the end of this venture, and he suspected it was because he was no longer willing to accept the falls of fate. He did not want this woman to be held in the inner courts of a Landlord. Because he wanted her himself? His eyes slid away from the dim, quiet form. There had been so many women; usually he was sure of his own intentions within minutes. But this Trader's daughter heated his interest more than his body—if she was a Trader's daughter.

"You do not think we can escape."

The voice was so quiet, so much a part of his thoughts, that Stoat's sensitive nerves did not quiver. He replied as quietly, almost as if he were talking to himself. "This range is very narrow and so close to the cup that it can be searched thoroughly. Besides, it is useless for our purpose. So close to the town, it was long ago hunted empty."

"But we never intended to stay here."

The utter calm of her voice, Stoat found, was making him sleepy. Trader's daughter? Trader's daughter? Alarm bells rang in his head and his eyes narrowed. Nonetheless, he spoke only of immediate practicalities. "But then I thought we would arouse little interest until after we had found or taken. I knew Vurn would report you and thought that if Vogel wanted you he would have taken you at once. Now I see the rationale in what he is doing."

"You are very protective." There was real warmth, perhaps even invitation, under the gentle laughter in Lahks' voice.

Stoat replied with a brief but picturesque obscenity, which he explained. "My own hide, and Shom's too, for that matter, are involved. Would it be safe for the Landlord to let us live?"

Lahks was silent for a bare moment, then said, "I have a comcov. Will that help?"

The hiss of breath drawn sharply between teeth described Stoat's surprised relief. The outgoing breath, however, was a discouraged sigh. "I doubt it. I don't think the Landlord has detection devices, but the droms will give us away unless you have a unit that will cover a lot of space."

"The droms? Do they work for the Landlords? Do you know anything about them?"

"No one knows anything about them. They stick out like a sore thumb on this planet, just like the heartstones; they don't belong here. Everything else on Wumeera is designed for the single purpose of killing something else so it can stay alive itself. The droms don't kill anything; at least no one has ever caught one at it. Yet they are indestructible."

"They would have to be, under the circumstances, wouldn't they? And their physical characteristics certainly mark them as indigenous. The skin..."

"You haven't really looked. The scales are set differently, the... Take it from me, they don't belong here. The important thing is that they follow people around. Helpful devils!

Whenever anyone wants to go anywhere, the droms are there. No one knows how they know. No one knows how to call them or send them away. When we are ready to leave tomorrow, they will be there. And out in the flats, their presence will betray us."

"If we do not move, how long will the search in this area continue? After all, we are in no hurry."

Stoat's eyes flicked at her and flicked away. "And your brother?"

"It will delay his rescue longer if I am caught than if I wait ... how long?"

"A day ... two ... I would let the parties pass twice. Even then they will circle the desert for days longer, but with luck ..."

"Will we need to use the comcov tonight?"

"Not at night, never."

"But ..."

"At night the heat-seekers walk: the crabs and silverfish in the deserts, the dragons in the hills. Why do you think we sleep in a stilltent?"

Lahks did not reply to the question because the answer was self-evident. If Wumeera predators hunted by detecting body heat, the stilltent, which conserved every calorie to be used for distillation of waste and exhaled moisture, was a superb camouflage. She reached into the small sack that held her personal belongings, then set the comcov between herself and Stoat.

"It needs only to set the projector and push the red button in."

It was unnecessary to say more. Whoever awoke first or heard something unusual first would activate the device. Stoat stared at it, all his suspicions alive, his nerves quivering anew. No comcov he knew was so small and compact.

The next two days were quiet. Stoat spent the time describing the local fauna, hunting techniques, and the most likely places for discovering heartstones. From time to time they fell silent as Landlord Vogel's men passed near enough to be heard or seen, but none of the searchers thought it necessary to test what seemed like a solid hillside for reality. On the third day the area was quiet. Toward afternoon, Stoat slipped out. Just before dark he returned to report that there was no sign of Vogel's men in the area. Lahks sat cross-legged, silent, her sudden need for activity as demanding as an itch.

"Tell me again about dragons," she said suddenly.

"They are large reptiles, carnivorous, hunt by temperature discrimination, are nocturnal... What do you want to know? I never counted their teeth or checked on the color of their eyes."

"Do they hunt singly or in packs?"

Stoat laughed harshly. "A single one is quite enough. Packs would eat each other. The only known association is during the breeding season, and even then only one of them usually walks away."

"There are three of us." Lahks considered, nodded. "Then we can move tonight."

The eyebrows shot upward on Stoat's lean face. "On the Russian principle of throwing one to the wolves when they get too close to the sled? One of us would hardly be a cavity-stopper to those little dears. All three of us might barely constitute an appetizer."

Lahks laughed and explained her idea. Stoat could not help grinning himself. "It might work," he mused. "I could fudge something." Suddenly his shoulders shook. "Trader's daughter, you are a lift to my spirit. I have walked a bitter round too long, doing the same thing in the same way. I had nearly forgotten a very old adage: There is more than one way to skin a cat."

"Will the droms come at night?" Lahks asked.

"Does it matter? They are no help against the dragons. They just stand and grin. And we will not be hunted by men at night."

"Skin a cat... skin a dragon. Contingent merchandise," Lahks reminded him. "We need transport for the hide."

Slowly Stoat shook his head. "This is no time to be a Trader. First, it is a full day's work to skin a dragon, even with the laser. Second, a dragon hunts alone, but the heat and maybe the smell, too, of the skinning would bring others of its kind down upon us."

As if to indicate that he would not argue the subject, Stoat moved across to where Shom sat silently, smiling vacuously at his companions. He opened a box containing explosive shells and another of small wireless detonators. These he fixed together, showed Shom, and told him to make others. Lahks immediately saw one reason why Stoat clung to his comrade. The idiot was extremely quick and deft. Before Stoat had finished cannibalizing an extra hotpak, a dozen small wave-controlled bombs were ready. Carefully, Stoat added a single heating element, showed Shom again what he wanted.

Lahks had not sat idle. When the booby traps were ready, everything was packed except the stilltent. Dressed in stillsuit under windsuit, each strapped on four bombs. Stoat stood for a moment, however, considering the last one.

"Perhaps I should go back along the trail and set this up to..."

"No," Lahks said firmly, not realizing until after the word was out of her mouth that, although there were good reasons for rejecting the idea, she had not been thinking of them. Her "no" had only protested against Stoat going alone into danger.

He frowned, then nodded agreement and hooked the bomb to his belt. "You are right, doubtless. There would not be time enough between the setting and the heating to take down the tent and get far enough away."

Lahks and Stoat shrugged into their packs, glanced briefly at each other, and slipped out of the tent. Outside the huge, low moon of Wumeera stood full in the sky. So near the desert, cloud cover or rain was not likely. Lahks was startled by the way the windsuits shone bright and suddenly understood why Stoat had laughed when she suggested night glasses. They would be visible from above for kilometers, she thought. She hoped Stoat had been right about the reluctance of the cup-dwellers to be abroad at night. She hoped, too, that the dragons would be more attracted to heat than to movement. Nonetheless, she trotted rapidly away to her lookout point, only taking the precaution of shrinking into the shadow of an overhanging rock. She made no attempt to watch behind and above her. That was Stoat's job, as it was hers to keep lookout behind and above him. Between them Shom stolidly collapsed the tent and folded it into a backpack.

The old world was so still that Lahks could see the air shimmer as the heat unabsorbed by the tent escaped. Shom stooped, placed the first bomb, and triggered its timer. Lahks strained her ears and eyes, although she knew that Shom's footsteps would cover any more distant sound, her laser ready. Their plan depended upon the dragons being far enough away to take at least fiveamin to get to the heat stimulus the tent had released. By then the bomb would be warm enough to attract. If they were as unintelligent, as responsive to instinct as most reptiles...

A twinkle at the curve of the depression in which they had sheltered themselves drew a bitter expletive from tense-tight lips. The laser beam, which cut steel like butter, broke into a coruscating blaze of visible light. Where it touched unbroken, rock glowed. Before the word had left her lips, Lahks had released the trigger. Unharmed, indifferent, three droms ambled placidly after Shom, bobbing their silly, grinning heads.

"Sorry," Lahks muttered contritely as she joined Stoat a few steps behind Shom. "I'm green and your horror stories seem to have sunk in deeper than I thought. Will that hot rock bring them any faster?"

A pointed canine caught by an errant shaft of moonlight glittered briefly under Stoat's face plate so that Lahks knew he was smiling or laughing. "It still depends on the distance they start from. Perhaps it's as well. I don't think you really believed that laser wouldn't touch these devils. Now you know."

"I still don't believe it. I've seen it, but... Should we ride the droms since they're here?"

"No. You can't hurry a drom. If we run, they will keep up—Yahweh knows why—but you can't prod them into moving faster on their own. We might..."

His voice checked. Shom had stopped, head cocked to the side. His hand rose, pointing a little to the left up ahead. Lahks knew her responses were swift, but Stoat reacted like his namesake. He was off to the right, where a splotch of darkness promised rocks. Shom, surprisingly quick for his bulk, was not far behind. Lahks took to her heels, her trained body making nothing of the distance between them. They dropped into the shadow simultaneously. The droms stood for a moment as if confused, then ambled slowly toward them.

Lahks repeated her expletive more softly, but with equal fervor, then added, "Damn them, they'll attract..."

Stoat laid his free hand on her arm and shook his head. The laser in his other hand pointed steadily in the direction from which Lahks could now identify the very faint crunch and slither of a large moving body. She had thought her ears were good but Shom's were far better, or else he had a sensitivity that went deeper. Stoat now turned his head toward the idiot, speaking softly but with single-word distinctness.

"Shoot it in the mouth, Shom. When it opens its mouth only. Right in the mouth."

A soft breath exploded from between Lahks' lips, and her body shook. The feral face whipped back toward her, and the free hand moved with the swiftness of a striking animal, but Lahks had already dodged slightly. She caught Stoat's wrist.

"Sorry," she murmured, "it struck me funny. I'm not hysterical. Sure we shouldn't wait for the whites of their eyes?"

The shadows of hood and face plate were too deep to see into, but Lahks felt wary eyes check the rise and fall of her breathing, the steadiness of the laser in her hand.

"They don't have any whites."

The remark could have been a flat statement of fact, but Lahks again got the clear impression of laughter. She giggled silently, then gestured toward the droms squatting in a semicircle around them grinning, bobbing their heads, and at times reaching forward to prod them gently with a snout. But Stoat paid no attention. He was straining forward, peering between two drom hulks. Lahks judged angle and distance, picked up the flicker, then the shine of moonlight on the body coming around a curve of hillside some distance away. Her breath hissed out again—but not with amusement.

Brontosaurus, but lean and agile-looking, with a horrible Allosaurus' head perched atop a thickened, yet still sinuous, neck. But, blessedly, that head was not raised and swinging. Neck thrust out, black-pitted heat sensors wide, seemingly blind to all else, the hunter was headed toward the trap. That was good and not so good. They had run off to the right, but the path they had originally traveled had curved slightly to take advantage of easier ground. As the monster came closer, even Lahks' practiced eye could not determine whether it would walk right into them or go by a hair's breadth on the left.

Instinctively, all shrank deeper into the shadow, but the rock was convex rather than concave and offered no shelter. Lahks thought she could feel the ground tremble, although she knew the beast was not that large. Five hundred meters, three hundred... Now it was impossible to tell whether the outthrust head was still seeking the heat trap or was fixed upon them, so direct was its angle. One hundred meters... Three elbows braced simultaneously on three knees; three laser pistols lifted across three wrists, as in a well-rehearsed ballet. Six eyes unaware of the harmony of motion stared, waiting for the glimmer of silver teeth in a mauve cavern, watching for the split-second when three fingers could trigger a burning light to discourage?, drive away?, wound?, kill? an invincible enemy.

Ten meters...But the mouth did not open. Lahks shifted the laser infinitesimally to bring it to bear on a heat sensor. That would penetrate, perhaps sting. Only, did the beast have nerves? And then, just as it seemed the head would top them and it would be too late to fire, the angle changed, changed further. It was swinging away. Without appearing to notice them, the dragon was avoiding the semicircle of droms, which had not even glanced backward or changed their idiotic grins for a moment.

Three long breaths sighed out. Somewhere in the back of her mind Lahks noted that Shom was not such an idiot as to have lost a sense of danger or self-preservation. What she said, however, was, "Are you sure the droms didn't help? The dragon avoided them."

Stoat holstered his laser, his eyes following the retreating form of the saurian. "I don't know. The droms accompany everyone and plenty of hunters don't come back. I was told the droms were no help. You want to try trusting them?"

Lahks laughed. "I'd love to, but a failure of the theory would be so very final."

"Yet to that finality the fortunate all come in the end."

A little surprised at the strange wording and the fatalistic calm of Stoat's tone, Lahks turned from watching the glitter of the moon on the dragon's scales to peer at his shadowed face. "True, but I intend to let the end be as far from the beginning as possible."

"I, too." There was laughter in Stoat's voice again. "And a steady courage, such as yours, Trader's daughter, can do much to prolong the middle."

Although she knew he could not see, Lahks' brows shot up. "We are well matched, then, all three. But we had better move on. Even if the beast takes the bait, who knows what may come of it? If it is only wounded, it may run mad."

They were about to stand up and suit action to the words when a dull "whump" from the direction in which they had come froze them. Stoat shook his head in negation of the question Lahks had not asked. He had not triggered the grenade, nor had its time-delay run out so that it triggered itself. Perhaps the impact of the dragon's teeth had set it off. But there had been no squall of pain. Lahks felt a flicker of relief. She killed, when necessary, swiftly and without a second thought, but she did not like to inflict pain   particularly on a dumb beast. If its head had been blown off ... Lahks thought doubtfully of the size of that head and the power of the bomb and realized as she thought that, if they had heard the explosion, they must have heard a body of that size fall.

If the beast were frightened by the explosion, would it become immobile or run? Frankly, Lahks could not imagine the dragon being frightened by anything, except another of its own kind. It was too big and also too stupid. One needed brains to be afraid. Still, she had opened her mouth to ask Stoat which unlikelihood was more likely when she saw his laser come up and then heard the beast herself.

Had she been alone, Lahks knew she would have been in no danger. To drop her temperature to where she was uninviting, to remain so completely immobile that the dragon's low intelligence would take her for a rock or stump, would have been possible. Now it was entirely likely she would be snapped up unnoticed with two other tasty tidbits.

Chapter

7

Fortunately for all three tasty tidbits, the dragon was no longer hunting. Where heat sensors had flared wide, flaps had dropped so that the great head presented a uniform silvery appearance. What was more, it presented a totally satisfied expression. Lahks could feel her eyes widening with disbelief. Of course, she had never seen the expression of a completely satisfied Allosaurus before, but if this was not it, what could it be?

The dragon's eyes were half-closed; the mouth, tight with tension when it had been hunting, sagged slightly open to display the point of a tongue from which a thick saliva drooled; the gait, previously lithe and purposeful, seemed somewhat uncertain. In fact, it looked . . . Before the thought could be finished, all three were crouching as flat against their boulder as possible. A drunken, staggering dragon might not mean them any harm, but to be trod upon would be as final as being eaten.

It could not be what she imagined. Lahks turned toward Stoat, leaning close so that she could keep her voice low. At that distance she could see in the dim light reflected from the rocks that Stoat's face mirrored the expression she had felt on her own.

"Is it wounded and dying?" she asked.

"Wounded?" he whispered furiously. "The damned thing doesn't even have indigestion. It liked it!"

The indignation in his voice tickled Lahks. In her effort to resist giggling, her tone was unnaturally grave. "Its heat sensors were closed. That means it isn't hunting anymore." Suddenly humor was intensified by a delightful notion. "Stoat!" she exclaimed with a broad grin. "You did tell me there was a rumor that the things actually breathe fire, that their breath is extremely hot?"

"That's why they're called dragons, yes, but it's imposs——. Wait a bit. On an oxygen-atmosphere planet everything lives by oxidation—that is, by burning fuel. We do it indirectly, and suitable fuel is limited to those things that fit our enzyme systems. But if we were tough enough to have a fire in our bellies..."

"Then anything burnable at the temperature of that fire would be fuel," Lahks finished for him. She laughed softly. "I wondered how any number of carnivores that big could exist where there was so little to prey upon. But they aren't really carnivores. They eat anything oxidizable at their digestive temperatures."

"But they prefer meat and fat because it burns slower and hotter—sure, and because they must have a subsidiary system to provide chemicals for growth and repair...unless they are a biological miracle that converts energy to mass——. By the Power, I'm ready to believe anything. Still, that bomb must have been hotter than any internal temperature."

"So, what? You can set oil afire with an alcohol burner and the oil burns hotter than the original flame. They must have a mechanism for carrying the heat away and distributing it, just as we have. Now all we need to know is how long that many calories will keep the beast contented."

Stoat shook his head. "I can figure the caloric value of the bomb, but I don't know anything about the dragon's metabolism or its usual intake."

A drom leaned forward and nudged Lahks. She rose, stared around. "Look, there's some higher ground ahead that looks as if it might provide shelter. We could go to earth there, set another bomb, and watch."

"Do you think you can tell one dragon from another?"

"Not unless they're markedly different in size, but you said they were loners, not gregarious. We'll know what direction it comes from."

On his feet, too, Stoat looked toward the area Lahks had noticed, then swung slowly. The ridge she had seen, silvered in places by the old moon, continued in a rough semicircle for some distance. The light was deceptive because Stoat, like the cup-dwellers, had lost the habit of traveling in the dark. He judged it to be about a kilometer to the crest.

"I would guess," he said slowly, "that the area inside that ridge is this fellow's territory. We were pretty central, which might be why he showed up so soon. Let's try for that ridge, see if we can find cover, and set our bomb. If the beastie doesn't show up, we can count on a good hour's traveling time for each bomb swallowed."

"But . . ." Lahks began. Then she said, "Oh, I see. The trap is a much higher heat stimulus than we are and might attract the dragon even if it wasn't too hungry. But, then what?"

They were already walking toward their objective and the full moonlight struck Stoat's face. A grin flickered across its feral intensity.

"I think," he replied, "that if this one doesn't take the bait and it goes off, the heat will attract the inhabitant of the next territory. If our luck holds, it probably won't dare invade, but it will be close to the ridge and hungry. If the ground slopes away on the other side, we can toss another bomb down. Even if the impact sets it off—which it shouldn't—it will draw the new dragon away from our direct path and give us time to set another bomb and get free."

The next morning found them still in the highlands but overlooking the lip of a desert that glittered in the rising sun. Lahks sat in her favorite cross-legged position chuckling quietly as Stoat, who was lying flat, laughed aloud. Both had been bottling up laughter for hours on end. In fact, they had studiously refrained from allowing their eyes to meet for fear of making unseemly noise. There was no sense in tempting even a drunken dragon, or anything else that roamed the hills, with shouts of laughter. There was something deeply satisfying in leaving a trail of totally contented creatures behind, as well as escaping.

Eventually Stoat stretched and turned his still-smiling face to Lahks. "Do we plan our next stage now or sleep first, Trader's daughter?"

"Tell me more tales of Wumeera while we eat. Then if nothing is certain, we can sleep on our problems. This world is so weird that dreams may provide better answers than thought."

Unfortunately the details Stoat furnished with regard to the desert fauna provided no new inspiration to Lahks. The silverfish were not too dangerous to a party equipped with lasers. They depended for protection against the wind and heat on overhanging carapaces covered with the same skin the dragons had. However, since their legs could be folded under the carapaces, these were not armored. They could be sliced off so that the creature was left helpless. Then it could be turned like a turtle and killed. The material of the windsuits came from silverfish, since the skin over the carapace stripped off readily.

Crabs were another problem altogether. They were not really a single animal at all, but a colony held together by a vitreous growth, which Lahks had seen used as windows. Unlike coral, which they resembled in some respects, the crabs had some sort of communication between individuals. If one saw food, the whole colony seemed to be aware of it and willing to move in the direction of the stimulus. These creatures were not resistant to lasers; however, killing one individual or even slicing the beast apart had no effect on the others. As long as one was alive, it strove to attack and eat.

The silverfish hunted by night, using heat sensors, as did the dragons; the crabs hunted more by day, but not exclusively. There was no certainty about how they sensed their prey, but Stoat thought it might be by vibration. They spent most of their time beneath the surface of the desert sands, but they always seemed to rise disastrously close to their victims.

At the end of a fruitless discussion, they all stretched out flat and slept. But when Lahks awoke, her first words continued, as if the talk had had no interruption.

"We made a mistake, I think," she murmured sleepily. "If the stones are farther out in the desert, we must be able to move more quickly. We need a flyer."

Stoat grinned. "I agree that we could use one, but would it not be easier if a heartstone grew legs and walked into the tent? That is equally likely."

"Not at all. A flyer was virtually offered to us, but, like fools, we hid instead of... ah, no, we did just right if... What is the likelihood that the Landlord will search in this direction?"

"There is some chance they will sweep it by flyer."

"And what would you have done if you knew the Landlord was after me, I was a complete fool, and you were thoroughly unscrupulous? Would you perhaps steal my goods, lead me in the wrong direction, and abandon me?"

Red flickered in Stoat's eyes. "I have fallen far," he spat, "but not that far. I . . ." His voice checked suddenly, he choked, and burst into laughter. "Yahweh save me from setting myself against a Trader. I have dealt with the Guild, but they, at least, think honestly of dishonesty."

Lahks' tilted eyes twinkled with amusement. "Because the Guild deals in illegal things, it must be reasonably honest to exist at all. A Trader is debarred from the high profit of stolen goods and illegal merchandise. Therefore, the thinking of a Trader is more . . . ah . . . flexible."

"Flexible," Stoat murmured, "that is a beautiful word."

He rose, stretched sinuously, and went to peer cautiously out of the tent, then left, with Shom following. The stillsuits took care of all bodily functions, but it was necessary to empty the dehydrated wastes from their receptacle. When they returned, Lahks went out in turn. She was beginning to feel distastefully gritty and dirty, but there was no help for that. Water was far too precious to be wasted on washing.

The light of the old sun was already reddening, although it was only an hour or so past midday, but there was no lack of heat. Without thinking, Lahks moved toward the shade of a low boulder. As she did so, it occurred to her that the boulder was incredibly black, far different from the ordinary rocks of the soil, and that its shape was peculiarly symmetrical. An artifact? If so, it was old, for the surface was deeply pitted. She moved closer.

The laser gun leaped into her hand as a tiny movement alerted her. After a moment, however, she drew closer still, and then still closer, holding the laser ready but feeling more curious than cautious. The air within a meter or two of the object was noticeably cooler, although she was still well outside of the small patch of shadow that it cast. With widening eyes Lahks circled the object, then holstered her gun and simply stared.

"Stoat," she called softly.

Before she had drawn another breath, he was in sight, a laser in one hand and a stunner in the other. With each passing moment Lahks was better pleased with her choice of partner. The integrity that awoke rage in him at the suggestion he might abandon a helpless comrade, the courage that brought instant response to danger, and the thoughtfulness that made him draw a stun-gun, as well as a laser, in case the threat did not require killing—all these delighted her. Perhaps . . . but that could wait.

"No danger," she said, "but come here."

Wisely, he did not holster his weapons. If she was the focus of an ambush and had been told what to say, so wary a hunter would not be caught.

"What do you make of that?" Lahks asked, pointing.

After repeating movements essentially like Lahks' own, Stoat said flatly, "I don't believe it. It isn't a rock. It's a drom. Only it looks like it's been solidified in some kind of tar with its head buried inside its body. But you can't hurt them—and no one would want to, anyway. Even homicidal maniacs like droms."

"I don't think it's hurt," Lahks said slowly. "I think it's . . . I guess you would have to say eating . . . although recharging might be more appropriate."

"But how can a living thing act like a solar battery? What does it do, turn itself inside out?"

Lahks shrugged. "Perhaps." Her eyes glowed with wonder. "You were right, of course. The droms don't belong here. They are artifacts—living artifacts. By all the Powers that Be, what sort of people could build such a thing? I must find them. I must know them."

Eyes and long canines gleaming, Stoat nodded in agreement. "Trader's daughter, I have been on Wumeera some five S-years, and in four days in your company I have learned more about this place than the natives know. When we have our heartstones— note that I say 'when,' no longer 'if'—and we go off-planet, will you consider permanent Contract with me?"

"Body or labor?" Lahks teased.

"Either or both!" Stoat responded promptly.

Lahks held out her hand, laughing. "When we go off-planet and you know the full tale of my woes, we will talk of it. But now we must get us a flyer."

Stoat gestured grandly toward the horizon. "Whistle, and

doubtless one will come down to you."

"Now, that is a very good idea," she said gravely. "I think we should do just that."

Again a momentary puzzlement in Stoat's eyes altered swiftly into comprehension. His thin lips pulled back in a rather mirthless grin. The robbery the Landlords had practiced upon him still rankled, and the hope that he would get his own back by the worth of a flyer gave him bitter pleasure.

"Certainly if I knew the Landlord wanted you, I would not desire that you be killed. I would want him to have you so that he would not pursue me. I would drug you, perhaps, and leave you your weapons and a distress caller. Shom and I can use the comcov to conceal us. I think the caller will cover its field even if they have a detect." Suddenly his grin faded and he hooked his lower lip with a sharp tooth. "But the damned droms will give us away. If those in the flyer see three droms, they will know you are not alone."

"If you ride, the comcov will cover you and them."

"Yes, but you can't stop them or steer them. How do I know what my psyche will want to do when I see the flyer? Remember, those idiot beasts don't read minds, they read the ego's, or maybe it's the id's, intentions." He paused, looking shocked. "Do you realize, Trader's daughter, that a people who designed such a creature had either no id or no superego? They had no conflict between desire and intention!" This time it was Stoat's eyes that grew round with wonder. "Trader's daughter, if you go to seek out these people, I will follow you with or without Contract."

"If they still exist." Lahks looked at the reddening sun. "This is an old planet, much older even than Terra, I think." She shook herself briskly, as if to shed physically the sense of melancholy her words had engendered. "But first things first. Why should the presence of extra droms betray us? Many came with a few men to the landing field."

Stoat shook his head. "You were impressed with the droms and did not notice the men. There was one for each man only. It is always so."

Lahks pursed her lips, plucked at them, frowned. "Do you remember when we hid from the first dragon? The droms sat near us and tried to make us move. If we set ourselves some forty or fifty meters apart, would two stay with you and one with me?"

"That is long range for a stunner," Stoat protested, "and I would not want to hurt the men. They only do as they are ordered."

"I do not think there will be any need to hurt anyone," Lahks said, giggling slyly. "Remember, such maneuvers are not unknown to Trade. But we must wait for morning. Listen."

Chapter

8

In the early light of morning, Lahks took a last look around to convince herself that all was ready. A bedroll, untidily open, many tracks leading away, but not far away, and returning erratically, a couple of spots that looked as if someone had thrown herself or fallen to the sand—all gave pathetic evidence of abandonment, search, and fear. Incidentally the disturbance of the desert sand also covered any tracks Stoat and Shom may have made and any signs of the extra droms.

Lahks glanced toward a slight hollow some seventy meters in the distance. It was farther than they had wished, but at any closer distance, the droms drew together, two facing toward the men and one, with dizzily swinging eyes (reproachful at both levels, Lahks thought), on her. She laughed aloud at the memory of Stoat's language and of a furious kick landed on a drom's flank that merely set the infuriated man hopping with pain without any effect whatsoever on the grinning, head-bobbing drom.

But at that distance even she, who knew where to look and what to look for, could see no sign of her companions. She flicked on the distress caller and flung herself face down on the bedroll, as if exhausted by effort and terror.

There was good reason to believe her wait would not be long. On a map scratched in the sand, Stoat had pointed out that they

71

were not far from the cup, having made a wide circle around it. The caller should reach a flyer if it was searching the central portion of the hilly ridge, or, at worst, if it was on its way home.

In the event it was well that the scene was set and ready, because response was quicker than Lahks had expected. Within a very brief time of casting herself down despondently, the distant hum of a flyer was perceptible. Lahks earnestly thought sad thoughts. She pictured herself as an abandoned orphan waif; she called to mind how much she missed Ghrey; she concentrated on the emptiness inside her when she had cut off Ghrey's communication. Soon tears were pouring down her face and her body was racked by the most convincing sobs. When the sound of the flyer forced itself past her concentration and rose above her whimpers of grief, she started, sat up, and stared. Leaping to her feet, Lahks ran toward the rapidly approaching machine, waving her arms wildly and screaming for help.

Inside the flyer the men smiled and sighed with heartfelt relief. They would be well rewarded for bringing home this prize and, from appearances, the prize would actually be grateful to them. Moreover, it would be blessedly easy. There would be no hunter to do away with—a breed notoriously hard to kill. Nor would they need to decide whether to make the woman hate them by destroying the idiot or endangering themselves by bringing him along. Wise hunter. Wise in the ways of the Landlords. He had abandoned the woman.

Then one said, "But if he wished to abandon her, why endanger himself by hiding with her for three days?"

The other laughed coarsely. "Are women so plentiful that he would not wish to sup off her before he ran?"

Shocked, but with his doubts removed, the younger man nodded agreement. Of course, a hunter would not care that the Landlord had claimed the woman. A flicker of longing for the freedom of a hunter's life was quenched immediately by his knowledge of the realities of hardship and danger—and there were no women at all in the deserts.

Within his bubble of concealment, Stoat cursed luridly, and Shom stirred uneasily under the impact of his emotion. Running toward the flyer that way might convince the men in it that she was glad to see them, but it would make them land so far from him that even the laser would lose accuracy. A renewed wave of suspicion—for Stoat no longer doubted either the nerve or intelligence of his companion—slid away into a feral grin of appreciation.

The Trader's daughter knew flyers. Since landing was a relatively long process—amin rather than secs—and since she had given every sign of being hysterical and foolish to boot, the men would be afraid she would run right into the machine. Naturally, they would overpass her and land well on the far side, knowing that her need to stop and turn would give them extra time. And that would force them much closer to where he and Shom were hiding.

However, that would also mean that the door the men opened would be on the side away from him. Stoat thumbed the stunner charge up to maximum, hoping both that the flyer did not sport sonic-resistant plexi and that the ship would be enclosed. He did not want to scramble any brains. He had another moment of anxiety when it looked as if the ship might set down right on top of them, but realized that the comcov had distorted his view a little. The flyer was definitely settling nearer than hoped. Stoat had lost sight of Lahks, but he was not worried about her; her only real moment of danger had already passed.

Lahks had recognized the peril, too. When the flyer passed overhead, she had thrown up her arms, as if to reach for it, flicking on all the electronic devices in her body at once in the hope that they would disrupt any stun-beam directed at her. None was, but the beeps, buzzes, clicks, honks, and wails of her own equipment responding to the myriad devices on the flyer nearly felled her. The panic-stop shut them off before any harm was done. Giggles now mixed with Lahks' sobs because she could not help appreciating how effective her stagger and shriek of dismay had been.

Arms still outstretched, she turned and began running back toward the landing flyer. Although her legs were pumping up and down at a great rate and much sand was flying, Lahks was not getting anywhere. She was pretty sure the men would not notice. It was a common effect to feel as if things on the ground were moving slowly after one had been skimming close to the earth in a fast-moving flyer.

When the door slid back and one of the flyer's occupants began to walk toward her, Lahks started to pick up speed, screaming hysterically all the while. The man called to her comfortingly, and then, moved by her distress, he began to hurry himself. Now Lahks was running all out, rapidly attaining the velocity of a small guided missile. At the last moment, a vague glimmering of doubt seemed to touch the Wumeerian. He stopped and tried to sidestep. It was too late. As if she also realized a collision was imminent, Lahks, too, changed direction but to the same side as her unfortunate opponent. She met him with the impact of a cannonball, at the very last second folding her arms so that she would merely knock the breath from him rather than kill by rupturing all his internal organs.

They went down together, rolling in the sand, giving every appearance of a man struggling with a hysterical woman whom he did not wish to hurt. The remaining occupant of the flyer, who had been watching the scene intently, half-rose and shook his head. It was the last voluntary movement he made for some hours. Under cover of Lahks' play-acting, Stoat had crept from the comcov's shield right up to the flyer. He was taking little risk because he could fire the moment the man's head turned in his direction. In rising, however, the pilot presented a perfect target. Stoat's stunner promptly sent him into a quiet, curled heap. As soon as he dropped, Stoat ran to Lahks' bedroll to shut off the distress call. The last thing they wanted was a second flyer. With that silenced, he returned to the machine and climbed in. There he stood and laughed aloud before he called, "Clear here!" through the open door and then directed Shom to go and pick up Lahks' victim.

"That was funny," he said as Lahks arrived, dusting the sand from her windsuit, "very funny. Our sleeping friend here was so absorbed, I could have climbed in with him."

"On a planet where there is a male-dominant society," Lahks replied, laughing also, "even when a thing should be suspicious to them, if a woman does it they will not let themselves suspect danger."

"It does not irk you, I see, Trader's daughter."

"Only a fool is irked by something that brings her advantage." Lahks looked around at their prize. It seemed in good condition, though very old-fashioned. "Can you pilot it?" she asked. Given time, Lahks could figure out the controls, and that would be natural-enough knowledge for a Trader's daughter, but she did not wish to waste either time or, more important, fuel.

There was a brief hesitation and an odd shadow passed behind Stoat's eyes, but at last he said, "Yes, long ago, very long ago, I flew such a machine. There is little I have not done at one time or another, Trader's daughter."

With a grunt, Shom heaved the man Lahks had left unconscious into the flyer. Stoat told him to bring the packs and the comcov. When he turned back to Lahks, the shadow had passed from his face and he was smiling again.

"Well, you have whistled and caught us a flyer. What miracle would you like to work next?"

"I must think about it," she replied with such gravity that Stoat was snared again and turned to stare. "After all, if I pick the wrong one and it doesn't work, you will lose faith in me."

A fine brow quirked upward. "Trade must be a merry way of life if there are many like you in it," he said dryly. "Meanwhile, what are we to do with these men?"

Shom had shut off the comcov and Lahks watched him gather their equipment. "How much fuel have we?" she asked.

Stoat slid sinuously into the pilot's seat, studied the panel, flipped a switch, then sighed. "Your miracle is perfect, Trader's daughter. The power is all but full."

"So it worked as we planned. They had just started and planned to go far afield. I think"—her lips quirked—"that since they have been so cooperative, we should save them a long walk. Let us drop them near the cup."

"No." Stoat's voice was positive. "A little nearer if you like, but neither will sleep long. We wish to be well away before they return to the Landlord and tell their tale. Besides, this flyer was not meant for the load we must carry. They have their weapons, and they were born on this planet. They can ride the droms home."

Lahks did not argue. She had sufficient confidence in Stoat's consideration for his fellow man and knowledge of the situation to rely upon his judgment. They deposited the original pilot and his companion in the small cave they had used as a campsite. Lahks left a note saying the flyer would be returned or its worth repaid. The men could use it if they thought it would mitigate the Landlord's wrath. Then they were free. Shom squatted with their packs in the carrying compartment. Lahks turned bright eyes on her pilot, who, after initial caution, was handling his craft with surprising dexterity.

"Where to?" she asked.

"Men have been on this planet a long time, long enough that some history has turned to legend and some legend to history. In the histories it says that when men first came there were ruins. They were very old, however, and so much decayed that nothing of the civilization that built them could be disclosed."

Lahks nodded. It never occurred to her that Stoat had introduced an irrelevant topic. In fact, she could almost guess what the introduction would lead to. However, since she was interested and there was no hurry, she did not intrude her guess.

"More likely the settlers had neither time, skill, nor energy for archaeological studies. This was an incredibly harsh planet. They used anything they could, dressed stone and such, from the ruins and ignored or flattened the rest. I have spent considerable time trying to pinpoint any place ruins were said to exist, however."

The sly-hot eyes flicked at her, and Lahks nodded again. "Because where the ruins were, the heartstones are found."

"So it seems to me, although I have nothing that could be called proof. Correlating a vague legend that there once was a ruin in such-and-such a place with an equally vague rumor that such-and-such a hunter found a stone near there is scarcely proof."

"A candle is better than no light at all on a dark night."

"There is a legend that in the heart of the southern desert there are great ruins."

His voice was soft, with a hint of longing, and Lahks did not break the silence that fell after he spoke. The ship hissed through the furious air, the low whine of its engine drowned in the total sound. Lahks, protected by her windsuit, had become so accustomed to the howling gale that was considered a quiet day in all flat areas that she was at first surprised at the noise. Stoat's eyes flicked continuously from fuel gauge to altimeter to distance gauge. Then he took the flyer up very nearly to its limit in altitude and repeated the testing process.

When he turned to Lahks, Stoat's face was devoid of expression, but Shom moved restlessly among the packs. Lahks would have liked to look at the idiot to determine the emotion Stoat was concealing, but it would have been too obvious.

"No one knows the extent of the southern desert, nor have I any certain idea of the place of the ruins—if there are ruins. If we could find them, there might not be fuel enough to return. There may not even be droms so far into the desert. Beyond that is the question of wind. If a windstorm catches the flyer in the air, we are dead. On the ground we might survive, but the flyer would be destroyed—and that might finish us, too."

For a long moment Lahks studied the carefully neutral face, the feral light of the dark eyes banked to deliberate dullness. Her lips twitched and then her merry laugh mocked the howl of the wind.

"We cannot control the wind. That might come upon us anywhere. The droms do not matter—we can walk. As for the fuel, we need not consider it until it is half gone. Hunter, you could list a thousand dangers more sure than those that threaten. When you breathed the word of untouched ruins..." Her eyes alight, Lahks laughed again. "A stone to buy my brother back. A stone to pay your labor. A stone clumsily hidden for the Landlords to find. A stone more, and my father's ship is free. What danger would I not dare for that?"

Chapter

9

The ridge of hills ran south, and Stoat clung to them all that day. In the late afternoon they found a tiny uninhabited cup and set the flyer down. The cups were like another world. This one could have been any peaceful valley on any planet. Plants grew; insects buzzed. In the brush a rustling and a flicker of white told of a small creature alarmed and fleeing.

"If you will set up our tent, I will bring supper," Stoat said, and disappeared with Shom at his heels.

In a short time he was back, two rabbit-like creatures, already gutted, hanging limp at his belt, and a variety of roots and other vegetables in his hand. Shom followed carrying a collapsible pail slopping full of clear, fresh water. Lahks looked from one to the other.

"I do not understand," she remarked as Stoat set up a heating unit and began to cook his prey. "Here there is game, edible plants, good water, and you do not need precautions against dragons. Why are there no people?"

"Too small." Stoat swallowed hungrily as the savory smell of his stew made his mouth water. Pack rations would last for months, were complete and sustaining, but they had neither taste nor odor and men still hungered for meat. "For a day, perhaps even for a week, this cup could support us. Then it would be bare. For a man alone, if he were very careful, it might be possible to live, but most men are not that careful, nor are they creatures who can live alone. Landlord Vogel's cup was once like this. Although it was much, much larger and the men were much fewer when they came, it was soon empty, as you saw it. The vegetables you ate in Fanny's hotel are ponics; the protein is vat-cultured."

"But this type of rodent," Lahks protested, gesturing toward the skins, "is a prolific breeder wherever it appears."

"I do not know why the animals are so slow to breed and the plants so slow to grow." He smiled slightly, as if at a private joke. "But I think, perhaps, that the planet is tired, old and tired."

"But why do the dragons avoid these places? There is no barrier to them. Even if old ones have established territories, the young must need living space."

Stoat shrugged. "Would you believe in magic?" he suggested in a faintly humorous voice, but with a basically serious intention. "It is the most logical explanation I can offer. No predator ever enters a cup, yet the droms pass in and out, and any domestic animal can also do so without discomfort."

"So?" Lahks allowed her eyes to wander over their small haven and then nodded. "Did he who made the drom make thee?" She opened her mouth to say something else, then leaped to her feet. "Where is Shom?"

Gratitude and deep warmth showed in Stoat's eyes because few would care what happened to the defective, but he replied prosaically, "Washing. There is a spring in a depression beyond the bracken."

"Well, thank the Powers—or whoever made this place   for that. I'll go and ..."

"Not while Shom is there."

Because her father had shed it completely together with the fanatical religion of the Shomir, Lahks had forgotten their excessive prudery. She realized her mistake before Stoat spoke, however, and raised an eyebrow icily. "... remove my windsuit," she continued, as if he had not spoken, "so that I can finish quickly. My mother and brother are Shomir."

She was beginning to be sorry for the lie because she trusted Stoat, but her urge to lay hands upon a heartstone was growing stronger. She did not want to take the chance of upsetting the smooth functioning of their team until that end was accomplished. Then at least part of the truth might be told. Now, however, as she rose to suit her action to words, she was reminded of what she had been about to say before concern for Shom had interrupted her.

"If this is an artifact also, should there be stones here?"

"Not now," Stoat replied positively. His voice was quiet but rage flickered in his eyes for a moment.

Lahks understood and pursued that subject no further. Instead, she said eagerly, "There are ruins here?"

There was a long silence. Stoat seemed to find the bubbling of his stew inordinately fascinating. Lahks waited, wondering. If there was something Stoat wished to conceal, he need only have answered "no" to her question. Therefore, there was something he wanted, but was afraid, to share. As if in confirmation, he rose without looking at her and walked away. Equally silent, Lahks followed across the cup.

On the far side, near where the sheltering hills rose, were what seemed to be shoulder-high bushes. When she came to them, however, Lahks saw they were trees, entirely perfect in form and shape and of species common on many oxygen planets; only here they were shoulder-high, whereas naturally they grew to some ten or fifteen meters in height. Lahks put out a finger and touched. They were real, growing, dying—she could see that some had fallen and saplings were rising in the open spaces.

Stoat was threading his way carefully through the miniature forest. At a trickle of water, which Lahks realized would be a moderate-sized stream on the scale of the trees, he stopped and turned his head. Looking in the same direction, Lahks gasped. Far from a ruin, perfect, of incredible, fragile beauty, a house waited. The evening sun glinted from little windows, glanced from the polished tiles of peaked roof and delicate towers, warmed the yellow stone to gold. The house exuded welcome, begged them to be small, to come in and live in joy. Tears pricked Lahks' eyes.

"They should not have left it alone," she whispered brokenly. "It is still waiting for them."

"Yes, but it is not lonely. Time has no meaning here. A thousand S-years, ten thousand, a hundred thousand pass this place as an hour. We feel pain because we cannot accept what it offers." Stoat took a single step, touched the roof, then the facade, with gentle fingers. "The house is warm and content."

By mutual consent they turned away. At the campsite Lahks

broke the reflective silence. "But the droms were engineered, if our guess is right, for men of our own size—at least our size. Who..."

Stoat smiled quietly, as if at a distant, distant memory. "I think it is a child's toy—a doll's house. What little I have seen of other ruins..." He shook his head. "There is no use in trying to speak of them. Like this or the droms, you must see for yourself."

When they started the next morning, clean and well fed, it was with the fixed determination to find the legendary ruins. Stoat lifted the flyer to its maximum altitude and left the ridge of hills. All three wore distance lenses and studied the terrain, but the bare scoured rock showed no sign of ever having supported any life, however far in the past. They set down only when the light began to fail in the lee of a pile of boulders. All had burning eyes and aching heads, and the howl of the wind, the sandpaper scrape of grit on the flyer's sides, the cold and tasteless travel rations offered little comfort. Tomorrow, early, would bring the point of no return with respect to fuel. Neither Lahks nor Stoat mentioned this. In fact, they spoke as little as possible.

No one felt any better in the morning. They were exhausted from cramping and lack of sleep, and yet their bodies, accustomed to exercise, twitched from lack of activity. Sustabs were mouthed; water, body-warm and faintly tainted with the ammoniacal chemicals that could not be wholly removed, was sipped from stillsuit reservoirs. They took off again. Lahks noticed that Stoat did not glance at the fuel register. If she said the word, she knew he would turn back, but not until then. They flew on.

After a time Lahks found herself swallowing down a faint queasiness. The ground below them seemed to be moving. She shut her eyes, opened them. Still the ground moved in slow waves. Then she noticed that the direction in which the grit struck the ship had changed.

"The wind!" Stoat yelled to make himself heard. "This damned lunatic planet, I should have guessed. The wind is circular. It runs around inside the great mountain chains."

"Am I dizzy, or is the ground shifting?" Lahks shrieked in reply.

"I think it's the ground. Maybe loose rocks and pebbles down there." Now Stoat did glance at the fuel gauge. To land in that river of rolling stones would be certain death.

"Go on!" Lahks shouted. "If the wind is circular, it will be quiet in the center."

For reply, Stoat only laughed, but he turned the flyer even farther broadside to the gale. It slid sideways sickeningly, and he fought the controls, increasing the power to compensate. Lahks closed her eyes again. It was useless to stare into that tide of rock. Nothing could stand against it. Any structure would have been ground to powder and rolled along with the mass within weeks. Suddenly Lahks remembered the sensation of caution Ghrey had transmitted. She had associated it with the heartstone, but the heartstone came only from Wumeera. Did Ghrey know this planet? Did she dare call and ask for help? Dare open herself to the desires of the universe again? She shuddered, and as her mind shied away from the thought, a picture rose in it. A drom, grinning and nodding, stood across the stream from the little house and it was quiet, very quiet.

Awareness that the quiet was not all in her mind made Lahks open her eyes. Certainly the wind had fallen, although it still blew grit against the ship. Far ahead, here and there, irregular, sharp shapes shadowed what appeared to be a mist. Below sand dunes rolled almost as restlessly as the sea. I must have slept, Lahks thought, glancing at Stoat's gray, sweat-shined face. She did not speak because it was plain that he, too, had seen the shapes. The flyer was headed directly toward them.

The wind continued to lessen, but as they reached the mist they were buffeted upward and peppered anew with flying sand. Once it hit, they could see nothing. His lower lip pinched by sharp teeth, Stoat fought to keep their course. Here the wind did not blow steadily but breathed in irregular gusts with irrational ferocity. Now the ship was tossed upward, now fell sickeningly as the air current failed completely. Lahks could not see the ground at all.

The leaps up and down and the sideways buffeting decreased. For a few minutes at a time it was even possible to hear the whine of the straining motor. Finally the intermittent spattering of wind-borne particles was more like petulant spitting than like sandblasting. And then, at last, they were free. The sand dunes below lay still, except for a faint rippling of their surfaces, and ahead, in a wide depression, was.... Could a city be merrily insane? Could ruins be happily irresponsible?

Above the engine noise came a sound so unexpected that both Lahks and Stoat jumped. Shom was laughing aloud.

In spite of the need to conserve fuel, Stoat circled the ruins once. By the time they set down, they were all laughing. Ruins can be many things. Some are tragic, some are awe-inspiring, some are merely melancholy. Never before had any of them seen comical ones. Two things were perfectly clear to Lahks and Stoat. The first was that the funny effect was not caused by the wind, the wear of time, or any disaster. The second was that, in its prime, the ruined city must have been more than funny; it must have been hilarious.

It was not a large city—town was a better word perhaps a hundred constructions in all. There were no streets. Sometimes it was necessary to climb up and over part of a construction to get to another. Open spaces appeared hither and yon, but with no apparent connection with the buildings—although to call the weird and wonderful shapes by that word was stretching a point. There were delicate lacy towers sprouting from odd angles of a squat monstrosity. There were graceful spans leading to nothing at all. There were long, low structures, curling and coiling around other constructions of sometimes indefinable shapes. The conjunction of exquisite beauty and blatant, unashamed ugliness went beyond being shocking. It was ludicrous.

In a sense, of course, it was insane, but Lahks realized after they landed the flyer in one open space on the periphery and looked at the whole from ground level that her initial judgment was not correct. Insanity, even when the "sufferer" is happy in his delusions, has an aura of sickness about it. There was nothing at all unhealthy in this wacky jumble. It was as if the dwellers therein did not care. Nothing at all mattered, neither the form or color of neighboring structures, nor the cost of building, nor even the physical shape or size of the inhabitants.

Stoat stood gaping at a slender structure, perhaps four meters wide, that bent over, as if to be a semicircle, but never touched the ground on one side. In this the door—it had to be a door, even though its shape was a wriggling irregularity—was at the top of the curve, ten meters at least from any point of entry.

"Did they have wings?" he asked.

"Or no legs at all?" Lahks chuckled, staring off to the right at an oblong structure in which she would have to bend over double to live.

"And that, I suppose, was for a short, fat snake?"

The irony in Stoat's voice was met by a glance of cool consideration. "There are such varying forms," Lahks murmured, "and this planet is old, old."

"You mean a galactic headquarters?" Stoat shook his head in negation. "No, for several reasons. I do not think this planet could have supported such, even as long ago as this was built. This came here after the desert, I think. More important, the planet is placed wrong. Wumeera is not on the rim, but stars are thin here. Most significant, however—all these people saw the same way. One of the most variable attributes of all species— even evolutionary divergence on the same planet—is sight. We see what we must. Look at the colors. The shapes are mad, but the colors are all in the same spectrum. They were all the same species, but"—his lips curved in a surprisingly soft, affectionate smile—"they must have laughed all the time—at themselves, at each other, at the world, even at the universe around them."

"Say they laughed 'with' and I will agree."

Still smiling, Stoat nodded. "Laughed with, then." He glanced around. "Shall we start to search or set up camp?" he asked lazily.

Lips parted to say there was no hurry, Lahks suddenly felt a ripple of anxiety. She really did not wish to do anything. Her only impulse... no, impulse was too strong a word, it was too violent... her mild inclination was to sit down, or even lie down, and watch the endless mad patterns rise and fall, twist and turn, carrying eye and mind away into their laughable intricacy.

"Stoat," she said sharply, tearing her eyes from a bulbous object that sprouted what appeared to be lavender feathers on one curve and pale pink spikes with shocking green, loose tentacles on another, "there is danger here."

"No," he replied, his thin lips slightly curved, "I am sure neither crab nor silverfish will be found here. This is akin to the cups in that. It is defended by... by something."

Desperately, Lahks strove to keep her attention on Stoat. Just beyond his left ear the pattern that was no pattern stuck out an impossible blood-red zigzag from which spheres of yellow festooned with gray-green arrows and polka dots seemed to dangle, beguiling her into laughter. Somewhere deep inside a bubbling desire to be different, to shift as the structures shifted, to laugh, dance, sing, and play awoke in her. Shom was laughing again. She caught sight of him whirling about, making little dashes toward one building and then toward another.

"Come live with me and be my love/And we will all the pleasures prove," Stoat said suddenly.

Lahks tore her attention from a triangle perched on its apex, the points of its base supported on one side by what appeared to be striped pink-and-orange sausage curls and on the other by an electric-blue girder too thin to support anything. Stoat's expression gave her so sharp a pang of fear that her laughter died. She was not afraid because he looked amorous; at another time and place Lahks would welcome the sexuality that fulled his thin lips and brought a tinge of color to his dark face. It was his eyes; the feral light had all but left them. The lithe, hunting and hunted beast was turning into a lap dog.

"Look at me!" Lahks shrieked, and she raised her arms so that her hands acted as blinders for him while her upper arms blocked her own side vision. "We will die here, all of us, still laughing!" she cried.

Awareness flooded back, accompanied by a soul-wrenching misery that made Lahks gasp with empathetic pain. Heartbeat-brief, that misery was followed by a wave of red hate.

"A trap," Stoat snarled. "A trap millennia old, and I ... I fell into it."

"No, no, it is no trap—at least it was not meant to be by those who built it. When we were hungry we would have eaten, slept when we were sleepy, and ..."—a regretful smile—"... loved and laughed. But when our food ran out or the chemicals built up too high in our body water and poisoned us, we would die, but only because it would be too late to go, and perhaps, even then, we would be unwilling to leave this. The desert was almost certainly no barrier to those who lived here. Perhaps this was even fertile then. Who knows?"

"Meant or not, it is still a trap to us."

"Perhaps not. I have broken the compulsion and you are free of it."

"Only so long as I do not look. And I can feel it draw me." His mouth twisted. "I am hungry for laughter."

Lahks nodded. She had guessed that. "Then laugh. This was made to give pleasure. I do not think it will hold us now that we know   and are afraid. I can think of a safe test. Call Shom."

Stoat raised his voice. At first there was no reply and fear grew in them, but after a few minutes they heard the idiot's laughter as he approached. Despite their anxiety, both had to smile. It was good to hear a sound of happiness from Shom. Stoat told him firmly, insistently, to fetch a coil of rope from the packs in the flyer. Then they waited again, wondering if the joy would prove truly false, beguiling them into forgetfulness.

It seemed very long, but perhaps it was only fear stretching the secs into amin. Still, he did return with the rope, and Lahks gained confidence and dared to peer under her arm. The nonpattern exerted its influence; her lips curved, and laughter gurgled in her throat. Nonetheless, she did not forget her purpose. She told Stoat to take the rope from Shom and to fasten it around his waist.

"Now," she said, closing her eyes and dropping her hands from his face, "look. Go to the nearest . . . er . . . thing and search. I will wait a reasonable time, at least as long as it took us to be affected. Then I will call. If you come, if you have employed your time to good purpose, we will know we are safe."

Chapter

10

The city was not a trap. They had no more trouble, even though the buildings—they had to call the wild constructions something—were as irrational inside as out. Here and there a pile of discolored dust indicated that a piece of furniture had yielded to time. In a few cases, however, other, more durable, pieces remained. Occasionally Lahks and Stoat could assign a possible use for the odd-shaped items. Sometimes they could only laugh. They searched every building in the town that had a readily accessible entrance, but they found no stones.

Just before dark they set up the tent and ate. It was not easy to induce Shom to come away from the town, but once inside the tent he lapsed into his usual state of vacuous passivity. For Lahks and Stoat the effect did not wear off so quickly. Lahks was quieter than usual. Although she had not the ability, she had the strangest urge to grow a nose like a trunk, turn her hair into snakes, or sprout wings.

Stoat, on the other hand, was more talkative, describing other worlds he had lived on and adventures he had lived through. Although she was interested, Lahks at first listened with only half an ear. Attending to adventure stories does not need deep concentration. In a little while, however, a certain inconsistency struck her. She began to make mental notes, and soon it became very clear that no single lifetime could encompass the tales Stoat told.

Yet Stoat was no mere boaster seeking to enhance his own importance. Lahks watched him. His eyes stared steadily into the distance, lit by the passing emotion of each tale. Not once did they flicker to her to check on the impression he was making. The day-long laughter had tired—no, loosened—him. Even the underlying wariness of his most relaxed moments was gone now. He was speaking only the truth, Lahks decided. But what a truth!

A legend herself, Lahks had less difficulty than most in believing in the reality of other legends. And here, unless her deductions were wildly wrong—a most unusual situation for a Guardian—was another legend come to life. There were many names for it: the twice-born, the flying Dutchman, the wandering Jew—those accursed beings who lived life after life and remembered. Much fell into place. The skills and knowledge that were too much for a simple adventurer, the seemingly needless isolation on a planet where solitary wandering need not be explained, the depth of longing for a resting place exhibited in the cup of the little house, the terrible hunger for laughter—all could be explained by the curse of immortality. Not, of course, that these "immortals" could not die. Any fatal accident or disease could carry them off as easily as any other being. Simply, they did not die of old age.

The knowledge confirmed Lahks' desire to tell Stoat the truth, and she stretched luxuriously. She could tell it all now. By the pressure of necessity the—Lahks examined Stoat's dark face and chose the most appropriate legendary name—wandering Jew was a well of silence. Certainly for the period of time needed to find Ghrey, she would have the ideal companion. As soon as they found a stone, she would show him what Lahks Mhoss could be. She leaned forward as he came to the end of a tale and touched his hand.

"Let us sleep," she murmured. "Tomorrow we must try the impossible buildings."

That next day they worked as Lahks, who thought that she had experienced every physical effort a being could make, and Stoat, who had labored through many lifetimes, had never worked before. They shinnied up slipping ropes to gain entrances fit only for enormous birds. They crept along swaying spans a spider monkey would avoid to leap to shivering excrescences and enter by windows where no doors existed. They wriggled belly-flat through passages that were the only opening into immense halls seemingly suitable for giants. But they found no stones.

Nor did the city's effect wear off. When they should have been rubbed raw by frustration and anxiety, as well as shaken with fatigue, they remained in high spirits. It was true that occasionally they burst into laughter at dangerously unsuitable times, but they did not become so irrational that the danger did not check them. And in the evening, although both felt relaxed and joyful, as if they had spent the day in idle pleasure, they were able to discuss the situation logically, if not seriously.

"Perhaps there are none," Stoat said, voicing the worst at once. "I am sorry for your sake, Trader's daughter, but I am content for myself. I have stored laughter enough for...for a long time."

"If there were stones at the sites of other ruins..."

"I did not say there were. I said only that it seemed possible to me. Besides, from what I have read, these ruins are nothing at all like the others. Perhaps more than one race lived on this planet. I know that cultures differed widely. Here in the equatorial East, stone was much used, or, at least, it looks like stone." He hesitated, then said, "I have seen three blocks of building material said to be from ruins. Trader's daughter, there were no tool marks on that material. It was too big to be cast, and it was not cut or worked."

Their eyes met and Lahks sucked in her breath. "It was grown?"

Stoat shrugged. "I cannot prove it. I have never been able to master emotion enough to examine the little house, but..."

"Yes. Yes. It has the...the charisma of a thing once alive, like a pearl. Perhaps that is what twists the heart so."

He twitched away from that topic, as one twitches a sore away from a groping hand. "Far to the North, where the everlasting snow lies, there is an intact settlement. I have not seen this, only read of it. There the buildings were made completely of the crab carapaces. Some interior walls had been stained to provide privacy, I suppose...but what a people who have no conflict between id and ego need privacy for..."

"So far north, perhaps they needed dark to sleep in the summer."

Surprise lit Stoat's eyes, and then laughter. "The most commonplace idea is usually right. Well, but what is important is that no historical reference or legend ever even hints that there was anything to provoke mirth in the ruins. In fact, I believe their shape, when it could be determined, was well within the normal conventions for buildings. That is why I say we may have come on a fool's errand."

Lahks shook her head. "Stones or not, what we have found here is of infinite value." Her eyes lit. "Stoat, is there room for a ship to make planetfall within the quiet area? Think what a recreation area this would make if it could be exploited."

"Trader's daughter!" For the first time there was a hint of scorn in Stoat's voice when he used those words.

Again Lahks shook her head, but she laughed this time. "I was not thinking of the profit although, of course, it would be there. But think of the joy of making a profit and of being a public benefactor all at once." Then she grew more serious. "Nonetheless, I am not ready to give up. If the stones were precious, would they not be hidden?"

"I cannot even guess where. Buried? Surely we cannot hope to find them if that is true."

"Not unless we have some clue. Stoat, can you think of *any* rational use for *any* building we have seen?"

He burst into laughter. "No. Can you?"

"If you could vary your size and shape, even your body structure, wouldn't those buildings be fun? If you could be a tiny little creature running through those small passages and swell to a giant as you reached the great hall, would it tickle your fancy? If you could put forth wings and fly to the high doors, soar off the spans that end nowhere, dangle like a spider from a thread of your own spinning from the swaying, hanging bulbs, would it give you pleasure?"

"Changelings?" Stoat stared. "You think this is the home of the Changelings?"

"Home? No, they have no home." Lahks was perfectly positive, although she could not tell why.

"Have?" The question hissed. "You know that they still are?"

A brief terror washed through Lahks. For a heartbeat of time the city lost its humorous quality; its abandonment threatened the death of her people. Reassurance came from the pure application of common sense. Her mother had been alive a short while ago. It was too much of a coincidence that Zuhema should have been the last of her species.

"They are," she replied surely. Then she grinned slyly and said with mock innocence, "Legends cannot die."

For once Stoat was too taken up with an idea to be sensitive to the fear of exposure. Avidity was clear in his eyes. "The people with no conflict between id and ego? The Changelings?"

"No," Lahks answered slowly, "I do not think so, although they must have been kindred spirits. The Changelings never build anything permanent according to the legends. But if they touched here, if the people who built the indestructible drom liked them and built for them...isn't this what they would build?"

"Certainly it is possible. But if the stones were of the native race, then there will not be any here."

"Can you believe that? Having done so much, would this kind of people withhold their greatest pleasure-giving device?"

"Device?"

"It must be a device. No natural object could display such characteristics. In the universe strange things have been found, but anything that grew from the bones of a planet or was spewed from the heart of a sun displays a certain range of characteristics. Only devices made by beings defy the elementary patterns."

"So, even so if some cataclysm that did not touch the Changelings took this race, and the Changelings fled, would they not take their stones with them?"

"That I cannot answer, but I am not yet ready to give up the search."

"Nor I—at least not until we have covered every building. Tomorrow we must try again to get into that low thing. It may have been a storage depot of some sort. It is the only one that has no windows and a shut door. Silly of us. We should have tried harder there first."

"Perhaps," Lahks said, smiling, "we did not *wish* to find what we sought too quickly."

Stoat looked startled, then laughed. "I think you may be

right. Logic pointed its finger and we turned our backs." He reached out and touched the lamp to bring darkness to the tent. "I think we have had our fill of laughter. Logic rules tomorrow."

They came directly to the low, featureless rectangle the next morning prepared to force open the door. It was not necessary. Stoat set a crowbar into one crack and leaned back, and the door swung quietly open. Both drew breath sharply. A soft golden glow had sprung up in the small antechamber that faced them.

Incredulously, Stoat said, "There is still a source of power alive after all these years?"

"The sun," Lahks replied, mastering her own surprise. "The droms are sun-powered. Why not this?"

"But the cells would be..." He left that unfinished. If the droms were indestructible, why not cells?

They entered on hands and knees, rounded a screen that blocked the light from the inner area, and stopped, hoping their eyes would adjust to the darkness. The absolute black, however, could not be compensated for by any widening of human pupils, and Lahks groped sideways to make room for Stoat to pull his torch from his belt. Her hand touched the wall, slid. Where her fingers ran, light sprang up. Again both drew sharp breaths. Lahks crawled forward, sweeping her hand widely over the panel. More light showed, a delicate pink to contrast with the pale green previously displayed. Lahks giggled, then poked a finger sharply at the wall. Blue, bright, more intense, as if to indicate the greater force of her stroke, glowed in a point where her finger touched.

Stoat backed out, crossed to the other side of the screen, swept his hand across the wall. Pearly white looped and curled in the pattern he made. Lahks heard him chuckle, then saw the basic symbols for his name appear in mauve. He rose to his knees and swept his hands from the top to the bottom of the wall in a continuous motion. A soft yellow radiance followed, blending into a large block all aglow. Stoat moved squarely in front of the light. Lahks saw his silhouette narrow, then broaden. He had turned to face her.

"Can you see me?" he asked. "Because I can't see you—only when you cross the light. To me, the center of the room is as dark as ever."

"So it is. Well, then, these panels are not made for lighting. In fact, they are designed not to light the room. Why?"

"Could this be an art gallery? The attention of anyone in the room must surely be fixed on the walls."

Before she replied, Lahks drew her finger across one of the pink lines. Where she touched, it winked out. She lifted her hand, touched the area again, and pale pink glowed. Without lifting her hand she pressed harder; the color intensified.

"It may be, but why so small? On your knees, you reach the ceiling."

"Could that matter to people who can be whatever size they like?"

Lahks was not sure. Her own changes in size had always been minimal. "I don't know," she answered, "but I have a feeling that they must have had a standard form and size, and that size was fairly constant. Many, in fact, most of the rooms were quite compatible with our size—which, again, is very common for dominant oxygen-breathing creatures."

"And why did the door open today? I swear I pushed, pulled, and hammered hard enough two days ago."

"Because you were not ready?"

"You say the building is sentient?" Stoat snapped.

Lahks laughed. "It was you who told me that the cups were defended by magic. I suspect, though, that when you forced the crowbar into the crack, you loosened something. Probably all that pushing had its effect, too. Well, an art gallery is as good a place as any to keep treasures. Turn on the torch and let us look."

The white light reduced the glow of the panels from a delicate miracle that commanded attention to insignificance. Lahks' eye was caught at once by a structure centered in the room. For once, its purpose was perfectly obvious. It stood on legs to about sixty centimeters high, ran about two-thirds the length of the room, and had tiers, three high, of the most ordinary drawers with ordinary drawer pulls for opening. Aligned in front of this cabinet were chairs, again perfectly ordinary, except that they were very small, suitable for children about six to twelve years of age. The cabinet was about one meter deep and double.

Without comment, both Stoat and Lahks moved toward it, one on each side. Stoat set his torch upright on the top so that they could both see, although not too well. Almost simultaneously they opened the bottom drawers on each side. A pale dust, possibly the remnants of paper or cloth, coated the bottom. There was nothing else, although Lahks thought she heard a faint rattle when the drawer slid open. The drawer itself, Lahks wondered? She wiggled it. The faint rattle sounded again. She peered closer. A narrow track could be seen in the dust.

As Lahks reached for the torch, her fingers met Stoat's, bent on the same errand. Both had apparently noticed the same thing. Smiling, he came around the cabinet on his knees. Together they searched carefully. A tiny ball, the size of a young pea, much coated with dust, lay at the side of the drawer. Slowly Stoat took a pair of pincers from his belt.

"Until you are sure, Trader's daughter, it is best not to touch   if we have found what we seek."

The little ball was lifted. Lahks blew at the dust. A glimmer of light shone through the remaining coating, faded, then pulsed again. Both stared, silent, a little awed by a success they had not really believed in. Without further words they circled the cabinet together. In the other open drawer, another pea-sized ball lay. They did not touch this one. Stoat swallowed, then opened the drawer above slowly and carefully. This time there was no sound of rolling, but in the light of the torch a larger heartstone pulsed red, green, gold. Softly they closed that drawer, exchanged glances, and moved toward the center of the room. There they opened the top drawer of the central tier. Large as a hen's egg, the fourth stone glittered as it caught the light.

Chapter

11

Kneeling as if in prayer, Lahks and Stoat contemplated a treasure literally beyond calculation. If every drawer contained a stone, there were more here than all those presently known. Slowly Lahks raised a hand. Stoat caught her wrist.

"Think, Trader's daughter. Do you want to touch that? Think of Fanny, exiled from his people, bound to a life he must loathe because of the loss of one of these. Think of the fate of others...."

"Have you ever touched one?"

There was a long silence before Stoat said, "Yes."

Lahks smiled. "Why?"

Lips tight with disapproval, but unwilling to lie, Stoat said, "Because I had to know."

Lahks' laugh trilled through the dimness. "And I, also. But, tell me, what came of your touching?"

"I am not one of those to whom the stone speaks. Their beauty draws me, nothing else. But I have seen others who were worse affected than Fanny."

"Shom?"

"No. What I said of him was true." Stoat's mouth twisted with distaste. "Do you think I would use him like a dog, thinking his longing would sniff out stones?"

"I think no ill of you at all," Lahks replied gently. She

95

THE SPACE GUARDIAN

thought for a moment, then shrugged. Ghrey's caution had not
indicated deep danger. "I must," she replied simply. "If I did not,
I would die wondering."

She took the little ball from the pincers and rubbed the dust
from it between her fingers. Quickly its pale pink deepened to
rose. It warmed, cooled; a golden glow pricked by green
flickered inside. Instinctively, Lahks rolled it between her palms
for a moment, then opened her hands to stare at the pulsing gem.
She had the strangest sensation that something was crawling
through her brain and leaving tracks. The sensation was not
unpleasant; it tickled a little and made her want to laugh.

Well, of course, that was how one grew smaller and larger. It
was a simple thing. And the wide band that might have been
Ghrey's direction suddenly reappeared in her head, but
narrowed just as suddenly to a clear, pointed beam. She could go
to Ghrey directly, speak to Ghrey directly, anytime—only now it
was no longer necessary. The crawling stopped. The stone
pulsed steadily, a small, friendly light. Lahks smiled and handed
the little thing back to Stoat.

Before he could sigh with relief or speak, she had taken the
next larger one, rubbed it clean, and caressed it. Vaguely she was
aware of her companion's anxious frown, but the crawling
through her brain had started again. This was more complex, as
if a many-tentacled thing was pushing through soft but slightly
resistant material. The sensation was vaguely sensuous. The
great world inside her opened still further. She could melt, thaw,
resolve herself into a dew—if she wished.

This time she hardly waited for the pulsing of the stone to
steady before she replaced it in its drawer and moved hurriedly
down the room to reach the largest. A hard knot formed in her
head. Lahks felt a welling of panic. She had made a terrible
mistake. She tried to let go, but could not. She was out of the
range of the torch and Stoat could not see the agony of her
expression.

In the burning red heart of the stone, a brilliant silver point
gathered. It grew cold, colder. Lahks knew that it was gathering
its energies, drawing in upon itself, to release that energy in a
burst strong enough to overcome the resistance in her brain. Her
lips trembled, struggling to form a plea for help, but her voice
was as paralyzed as her mouth. She struggled to shut her eyes,
but the pupils remained fixed upon that pinpoint of light, now as

96

brilliant as a star, in the heart of the stone.

The knot in her head grew tighter. The light stabbed through her distended eyes, running needles of pain through her skull. It burst! Showers of light. Silver crawling with blue, gold, green. The knot burst. A thousand red-hot spears tore through her mind, shattering it to fragments. The colors bled into each other, rolled, twined, writhed. Her brain dissolved into mush, reformed in lumps, convulsed, twisted. Lahks screamed.

By the time Stoat reached her, Lahks was sitting cross-legged on the floor, giggling. She heard his agonized oath, struggled with herself, and managed to gasp, "I am all right."

"What happened?"

"I skipped a few lessons. I do not know when you last went to school, Twice-born, but you may remember that cramming for an exam is far more painful than studying steadily."

When her voice stopped, there was so intense a silence that she knew Stoat was holding his breath. Then it hissed out.

"Why do you call me Twice-born?"

The snarl of a desperate, cornered animal was in his voice, but Lahks did not flinch. Tenderly she touched his cheek.

"I will not ask for the secret," she said. "I know it is long lost, even to those who bear the curse—and I do not need it. Look. I, too, have a confession to make." She turned the torch on herself, insisting, "Look at me."

And slowly, before his eyes, the short brown hair lengthened, lifted, writhed, hissed. A hundred beady eyes glittered; fifty forked tongues flickered. Lahks' smiling face was crowned by Medusa's glory.

"That is a very clever trick," Stoat said tightly. "You are a hypnotist of no mean order."

"I am no hypnotist at all. They are quite real. Touch them. You know illusion has no substance. Come outside. I will grow wings and fly to one of the towers."

There was another breath-held silence, and then Stoat sighed. "No wonder you were so eager, so interested in these ruins, so sure of the Changeling's ways. Changeling! You are a Changeling!"

"I am now." Lahks giggled. "If you do not tell about me, I will keep silent about you. We are both among the damned of the universe."

The snakes coiled and hissed. Stoat said irritably, "For the sake of the six-pointed star, make hair again. I cannot think with those things wriggling about."

Agreeably, Lahks made hair. "Let us go out," she said, replacing the heartstone in its drawer. "My knees are sore from kneeling."

In the open she glanced at the town of her ancestors and broke into peals of laughter. Stoat watched with a touch of anxiety, but Lahks soon had sobered enough for conversation, and she sat down with her back resting against the building. Stoat sat beside her.

"So much mystery, so much research, all over so simple a thing. Those"—she pointed at the heartstone Stoat still held—"are only learning devices. Oh, they're complicated beyond anything—I think they are a single molecule—but they're not meant to be a mystery.

"You mean you know how to create a heartstone now?"

Lahks shook her head in quick negation. "No, no. Like your secret, Twice-born, that is lost, unless some of the makers still survive somewhere. My people never made these, although I suspect they may have inspired them. That"—she touched the stone with a forefinger—"does not teach. It only permits an integration of what one already knows or is being taught—not only an integration, but a drawing to the surface so that the conscious mind can use unconscious, even cellular-level, information."

Stoat looked suddenly startled and almost dropped the little stone. "That must be right. I said the stone I found did not touch me, but I was wrong. We . . ."—he hesitated, as if unsure of how to identify himself, and continued with wryly twisted lips—" . . . we wandering Jews are not immortal. Our span is long, but not forever. At each division the cells forget a little. When I came here, I was at last growing old. That was why I dared take Shom with me."

He hesitated again and Lahks touched his hand. "I understand. It tears the heart when the companion grows old. Once, twice, and you dare not love again. I said we were both accursed."

"Yes." He stared down at the pulsing pea. "But now . . . I noticed my old bones no longer ached, my eyes were clear again—after I touched the stone. I thought it had healing properties. I was wrong. I had relearned the pattern of regeneration. Perhaps"—his voice was very tired "perhaps I am now truly immortal." His eyes closed. "Yahweh, Yahweh," he whispered, "what shall I do?"

Lahks laughed. "Live this day in joy, for tomorrow the wind or rolling rocks may kill us. But if we do not die here, I have two keys to two separate doors. One is a place of pleasure, the other a workshop. You shall have your choice—or both—Twice-born."

Again Stoat's lips twisted. "Once born of woman, once of machine or test tube. I do not know. The secret was well kept. I did not even know I was among the chosen. One night I slept; I awakened a year later—Twice-born."

"Why?" Lahks asked curiously.

"Because before we—I mean the people of our native planet—sailed the stars and learned that anything that thinks is human and equal, not that all have learned that even now, my people—the Jews—were considered by many to be accursed or unclean or some such. From time to time the other peoples of the world tried to wipe them out and forever obliterate their—my—faith. There was a fear born in our bones—no, deeper, in our cells—that we would die out as a group. They were clever, my people, learned and clever, and many were rich. That was how they had survived the millennia of being hunted. While the secrets of the cell were being unraveled, they set themselves to rebraid those secrets into a cord of immortality. They succeeded. Then they weeded out those they considered unfit. The others were reborn—immortal."

"So your people did not die out?"

Stoat laughed. "Not at all. On our native planet they are many and prosperous. Indeed, they have spread to many worlds. They were always great travelers, although they set the blame for their wanderings on others and much bewailed the loss of a homeland. But not one of them is a Twice-born. They are the descendants of the dregs—those refused the 'blessed' rebirth into damnation."

"And the Twice-born?"

"I do not know." Stoat shuddered. "For a little time—a few hundred years—some effort was made to keep contact. After that ... Does one infected with a plague seek to take on another infection? Doubtless some like myself may still wander the universes, too unlucky to be killed by accident and too cowardly to end their own damnation."

Lahks' silver laugh trilled out. "Or too curious, except in moments of self-pity, to stop sticking their noses into the whys and wherefores of life. There are times when it is right and proper to die by one's own hand—but not because of boredom. I gather that the Twice-born learned their lesson?"

"Oh, yes. Within a few hundred years most of them were dead—by mischance, torture to discover a secret we did not know, or suicide. And the secret had been obliterated so completely—my people were conscious of the population problem [we had not then reached the stars] and did not wish to make a world immortal—that even the lines of research that led to the secret were wiped out so that the process could not be resurrected."

Lahks shook her head. "But doubtless it has been, from time to time, by others, and will be again."

Stoat ignored the philosophical remark. "What did you mean before when you said you had skipped a few lessons?"

"Did you realize that the building is a schoolhouse? The lighted panels were for some kind of lesson display, I suppose. The children sat in the chairs, watched the panels, and I guess they used the stones as an aid. The stones are graded in size for a purpose. Each increase ... well, I don't know how to describe it exactly, but let's say it opens new pathways in the brain. My experience with the first two was pleasant. Then I skipped to the largest and it had to do everything at once. Maybe that accounts for the evil effects on some people." She hesitated. "Are you going to try the larger ones?"

Stoat considered. "I could not resist any more than you. Think of the hell of wondering what I could have learned through all eternity. I guess I was lucky. My find was one of the very small ones. But it will take all of us to get out of here. I won't try now. Let's take one of each size, at least. If we escape and come to a safe place, I will try." He gripped Lahks' wrist and held her with his eyes. "If I am rendered mindless, you must destroy both Shom and me. That will be best for us and will leave you free of a burden."

Without hesitation, Lahks nodded agreement. His request was right and rational. When the intelligence was gone, the person was dead—no matter what the husk that remained did in the way of breathing, eating, and excreting.

"What is your true name, Changeling?"

"Lahks Mhoss. And yours, Twice-born?"

Stoat opened his mouth, closed it, and said with a puzzled smile, "I do not remember. I have used so many names over so many ages. No name I remember is more mine than Stoat."

"It suits you."

Their smiles met. "Yes." He was silent, relaxed. "Well, what now? That tale you told of seeking your brother was just a tale. What did you want a heartstone for?"

"For what it has given me—an understanding of myself. But the tale was mostly true; only it is my father that I was seeking, not my brother. Now we can go to him, if nothing more interesting bars our path and if you will come so far."

Still smiling, Stoat waved at the horizon. "Grow wings and fly us out of here and I will go to the end of the universe—or into new ones."

"You are quite right. Our next problem is indeed a way out. Will the flyer take us over the rolling rocks?"

Stoat shrugged. "I do not know. I fear not. The power is low and the wind there..." He shrugged again. It was not necessary to complete the statement.

Lahks consulted her more esoteric mental and physical equipment. The Guardian training had provided her with personal defense weapons, as various as they were efficient, and with the last word in communications devices, all neatly buried in various parts of her anatomy. The weapons were obviously of no help here, and the communicators connected only with a report center of a Guardian installation. That the Guardians might fish her out of fatal trouble was, of course, possible. However, it was very doubtful, indeed, that they would consider the situation she was in as dangerous, let alone "fatal." More important, Lahks had gone to considerable effort to shake free of her Guardian associations. Only in the last extremity would she contact them.

The Changeling heritage had made it possible for her to grow wings or turn into a mist. It did not, unfortunately, provide flying lessons or indicate what to do when the molecules of mist that had been Lahks were dissipated all over the area by hurricane winds. Beyond that, it would not help her companions. Since matter could not be created or destroyed—even by Changelings—the growth of wings would reduce the density of the rest of her body. This, although it would permit her to fly, would, on the one hand, make it impossible to lift any real weight, and, on the other, make her even more subject to the force of the wind.

"This is one time we need power to counter force," Lahks said at last. "The power of the mind, except for telekinesis or teleportation, is useless."

"I have been thinking the same thing," Stoat replied. "I know something of engineering, but even if I dared cannibalize every power source we have, it might not be enough. Also, this is a bad planet to be on without weapons."

"Except for the area of rolling rock, we could walk. Could a flyer be raised in a wind strong enough to shift sand?"

"Where there are no tall obstructions, I think so. The flyers depend on the air to lift and carry them. The power is used to give speed and direction, or if you wish to travel against the wind, for that." The edge of Stoat's lower lip slipped under his sharp canine. It was an expression of calculation that Lahks had not seen since they entered the laughing city. "If we could move the flyer past the up-and-down drafts into the band of steady circular wind, we might—I say *might*—cross the rolling rocks with the power supply we have."

For a long moment Lahks was silent at the thought of the gargantuan task. Then she sighed resignedly. Without further discussion they reentered the schoolhouse to gather a pair of each size stone. After some thought Lahks took two more extra tiny ones and a few of medium size.

"We will need them to buy our way free, and I would like to give one to Fanny, if we could find some way," she remarked. "This is no world for a gorl."

"It will do him no good," Stoat warned. "I have been thinking about that. You have no desire to keep stones. It has taught you, and you are finished with it. I, too, do not feel any craving— aside from curiosity—to keep or handle them. Perhaps if it cannot teach, it creates dreams or euphoria. That may not be healthy."

"Probably you are right, but Fanny's people can afford a nonproductive dreamer or two. Let him be happy."

Stoat raised an eyebrow but made no further protest, nor did he comment when Lahks slid the stones into her belt pouch. They went then to the flyer, where they considered the problem of getting it down off its landing skis. The rounded belly would make a good surface for dragging, if the abrasion did not rip it away.

Of course they had no jack to support the ship or let it down easily. However, if the main supporting struts of the skis were removed, the thin outer bracing struts would probably bend slowly under the weight of the flyer. Stoat tested them as well as he could to make sure they would bend slowly rather than collapse suddenly. When he was finished, he smiled wryly at Lahks.

"I know about as much now as I did before. I think it will work. Of course, I am not sure we can lift belly-flat, but maybe we can pry it up a bit with the skis if we have to."

"Give me a long-enough lever, a fulcrum to place it on, and I will lift the world," Lahks misquoted solemnly.

"It would help," Stoat replied, eyeing the skis with disfavor, "if the lever were strong enough not to bend." Then he turned to get tools from the flyer and his eye was caught by the panorama of the town. He smiled and shook his head. "It's still funny, but somehow it does not hold me now."

"Because it is not really irrational anymore? Because you know the people who used it?" She laughed, touched his arm. "You are a good immortal. The will to live is strong in you, you can still laugh, but beyond that you are still curious and, even more important, dissatisfied. The ages that have passed over you have not quelled your urge to dig up the Garden of Eden."

Surprised, Stoat turned to her. "You know the Book?"

"Yes, of course. It is still the best description of Homo sapiens—of his character, his desires, and his dreams—that has ever been compiled. It took about ten thousand Terra years to gather the knowledge, another five thousand to compile and codify it, and perhaps another one thousand to write it down. The information is of infinite value. In fact, it has given rise to a term that distinguishes Homo sapiens from all other animals and from most other intelligent species—The Garden-of-Eden Syndrome."

For a moment Stoat looked blank. Then understanding dawned and he began to chuckle. "Yes, I see. I see. Homo sapiens, like any living thing, will try to alter an unfavorable situation to suit him. But *only* Homo sapiens will destroy perfection, because even perfection cannot satisfy him." His eyes lit. "You are quite right. I still have an ineradicable impulse to dig up the Garden of Eden."

Lahks, also chuckling, nodded. "Me, too. It's the best evidence I have that I am only part Changeling. The Changelings will not even pull up weeds, not to mention disturb perfection. Besides," she added with a flash of mulish rebellion, "how can you tell what perfection is? If apparent perfection were changed, it might become more perfect."

"Perfection is a word with only an abstract meaning. It cannot exist in reality. Only Yahweh is perfect—the Nameless God—and, like perfection, His reality is open to question."

Stoat reached into the flyer and drew out the roll of tools with which he attacked the main struts. Handing wrenches and sometimes working on her own to balance the relaxation of the supports, Lahks considered what Stoat had said. He was, of course, quite right. Most intelligent races toyed at one time or another with the concept of an all-powerful, all-knowing, all-comprehending being that controlled fate. But among all the races of beings in all the eons the subject had been pursued, not one iota of proof had been obtained.

There were other similar concepts—justice, good, right—that had perfectly clear abstract meanings, but when dealt with or applied in reality, they degenerated immediately into their opposites. These, Lahks thought with a wry grin, always had very, very real existence.

That was why the Guardians had given up the whole question of right-wrong, justice-injustice, good-bad. The organization, indifferent alike to genocide and humanitarianism, was concerned only with the study of intelligence and the prevention of stasis. Initially organized to prevent one intelligent form of life from preying upon another—by mistake or intent—the Guardians soon realized that intelligent beings had a worse enemy than each other.

It was true that among the many races of the myriad worlds one or two intelligent life forms had been made extinct by another. (The unintelligent life forms were less fortunate; they were wiped out regularly by their big-brained rivals.) However, this was a totally insignificant problem compared with the thousands of intelligent types that had been destroyed by good—by Utopia.

It was part and parcel of that belief in the possibility of perfection Stoat had mentioned. Most intelligent life forms did not partake of Homo sapiens' insatiable desire for change. Once these people found a way of life they believed was perfect—a way of life that indeed satisfied everyone, left no one hungry or oppressed or deprived of emotional satisfactions—it became static. The next step was decay, a decay to which, however intelligent, the beings were blinded by the belief that they lived in perfection. Beyond that was death—the extinction of the intelligence of a whole species.

The Guardians guarded against just that—stasis. It mattered nothing to them whether a government was just or unjust, whether a people were happy or unhappy; if, over a certain long period, no change in social structure, scientific and technological level, or political type took place, the Guardians gave the culture a jog. The means they used often were not nice. The results they obtained sometimes made the merely amoral shudder and turn pale. Wars, they encouraged, and they winked at interstellar conquest; the death of millions, they shrugged off as irrelevant. Those who remained would need to redream their notion of perfection, to fight to drive off their conquerors, to strive again to rebuild their Utopia. And in the process they would regrip life. That particular intelligence with its unique qualities, whatever they were, would be preserved in the universe.

Of course, it took a warped mind to be a Guardian. Homo sapiens were much used, but their life-span was short and Guardian projects ran into millennia to finalize. Most people were not fitted by nature to destroy what seemed good in the interest of some long-distant and wholly questionable future. But Stoat—Lahks watched him fasten a leather strap to one main strut and move cautiously to the next—would fit in well. For one thing, he would be able to see the effects of Guardian interference. The life of races rather than individuals, with whom he dared not involve himself, should maintain his own interest in living—and hers. For Lahks now knew she too was nearly eternal—if the desert did not kill her tomorrow. Suddenly she laughed aloud and stepped aside to grasp one strap.

"Are you strong enough?" Stoat asked. "The pull has to be even."

Lahks laughed again and shrank half a meter. Her clothing

THE SPACE GUARDIAN

was now loose and uncomfortable, but she could feel her muscles knot like steel as their density increased. Stoat grinned, lifted his fingers in the cabalistic sign for luck. They counted off, matching rhythm.

Chapter

12

Although the flyer had come off its skis without serious damage and Stoat had contrived harnesses for all three of them from various ropes and strips of cloth and leather, it seemed for a time that they would not leave the Changeling town. Shom, usually so docile, had very nearly turned ugly when they tried to force him away. Even after the waves of empathic disapproval that flowed from Lahks and Stoat had cowed him, his grief had nearly shaken their resolve. Stoat found the solution to this problem. After several anguished moments of studying Shom's face, he said suddenly, "Give him a stone."

Lahks took a tiny bead from her belt rather doubtfully, brushed it clean, and held it out. "Look, Shom," she crooned, "look how pretty. As pretty as the houses, see?"

His glance flickered toward her, then turned back to the lodestone of his joy. Finally, Lahks took his hand and pressed the stone into it, folding his fingers over the gently pulsating warmth. In secs he opened his hand, but not to let the stone drop; he stared at it.

"Speak to him," Lahks murmured to Stoat. "Tell him we must go and what we must do."

"Shom," Stoat said loudly, clearly, and slowly, "we must leave here. There is no food or water. If we stay, we will die. We cannot use the flyer now. We must pull the flyer as far as we can—to where the sands are rolling."

Shom had not taken his eyes from the tiny heartstone, but Stoat and Lahks had both noticed the change in its rate of pulsation as he spoke. It was brighter, with sparkles of color playing on its surface. Shom stood placidly as Stoat harnessed him to the point of the flyer. Lahks took the left side, Stoat the right. The two exchanged worried glances. Shom still gave no sign that he would respond.

Stoat said, "Straight ahead, Shom, into the open." And then he gave the count. "One, two, pull!"

To their intense relief Shom flung himself forward on the word, just as they did. The flyer groaned. "Ease off," Stoat ordered. Then, "All right, one, two, pull!" This time the structural groan was accompanied by a scritch of metal on sand. Perhaps the machine had moved a millimeter. They backed up, breathed, pulled again, straining until the blood vessels bulged in neck and temple. More movement, and they were establishing a rhythm.

By the end of the day they were out of the town with the flyer in sand that had no firm base. Whether they could achieve their goal was still highly problematical. Now it was a race between the distance they could move and how long their food supply would hold out and the stillsuit refining of their waste body water would remain adequate. The flyer moved better in the soft sand than over the hard base, but it only moved by centimeters.

That night the silence was unbroken except by soft groans as muscles, strained beyond endurance, twitched and knotted. They had hardly eaten, although Stoat and Lahks realized that the food was essential for restoration. It was simply too hard to chew. Even Lahks' laughter was stilled; it hurt, and the effort was too great.

The morning was worse. Lahks whimpered with pain at every movement. Stoat lay with set lips staring at the roof of the tent. Shom was silent, sitting in his usual cross-legged position. Although he was staring at his tiny heartstone with a beatific smile on his face, Lahks did not like the grayish tinge of his complexion.

She took her own breakfast, noticing with growing depression that Stoat made no move toward the food. An immortal could grow very tired of life. If retaining that life grew unendurably hard, it might be very easy to give up. She searched for something to say that would restimulate him and instead found herself wondering why she was bothering. Where she had strained against the improvised harness, her flesh was swollen and purple. The very thought of donning that harness again made her cringe. That Lahks could shift the damaged tissue elsewhere, that it would heal with enormous rapidity, did little to ease the shock to her mind. Aside from that, what of Stoat and Shom? Could she drive them to further effort?

"Lahks," Stoat said softly, startling her because it was the first time he had used her name, "could you fly the winds?"

"No." Her reply was unhesitating. "There are no dwellers of the air on Wumeera. Therefore, nothing with wings can fly the winds."

He lay still some moments longer, then sat up, the lines on his face setting even harder. "Then there is no possibility of bringing in a ship to get us out." He shrugged fatalistically. "Tomorrow, when we are a little farther from the defended area, we will have to wait a day while I hunt. The silverfish are edible and the flesh will provide us with some fresh water."

His voice was completely matter-of-fact, and he reached for a food packet with one hand and for the harnesses with the other. As he chewed and swallowed, his fingers swiftly altered straps so that they would not touch bruised areas. Quite suddenly Lahks' infectious chuckle filled the tent. Shom looked up from his stone and laughed, too. Stoat's expressive brows climbed upward questioningly.

"Nothing," Lahks said, waving a hand negligently. "I was thinking of another legend. Eons ago there were men who built bridges and roads for the making of war—when wars were made upon the ground. Their motto was: 'The improbable we do immediately; the impossible takes a little longer.' You are plainly of their breed."

Stoat's lips twisted wryly. "Indeed, I am. They were men of the planet Terra." Then he sighed. "This task, I tell you, is one of those that will take a little longer."

Nonetheless, when he finished his meal he rose promptly, reattached the harness to the craft, and, when Shom and Lahks were set, began the count to get the flyer moving. They gained a centimeter, rested, threw themselves forward again, and, like a well-rehearsed comedy team, all three fell flat on their faces as the craft shot forward a full meter. Lahks scrambled to her feet, spitting sand, and shouted for Shom to get up as the flyer edged steadily ahead. Stoat was already up, moving on to keep out of the way but straining sideways in an attempt to see around the bulging side of the craft. His laser was free in one hand, and his other fumbled at the harness straps.

"What is it?" Lahks choked around the grit in her mouth.

Conceivably a crab could have gotten under the flyer and propelled it forward while trying to get at them, but nothing Stoat had said of them indicated they had any great strength. And even if the creature had caused the first forward surge, it would have sunk into the sand again and risen in a new place when it encountered such strong resistance.

"Beldame, your luck holds well," Stoat called. "There are three droms pushing."

"Is there enough material to harness them in front?"

"I don't know," Stoat replied, "but it doesn't matter. I am not sure we could direct them. Probably they would follow us, but they might have a set path we would not wish to travel." He slipped his own harness back on. "It will be safer to stay harnessed and change the direction when we like by pulling to one side or the other."

"How will we stop?"

Stoat laughed. "I am not sure. I think if we stop, they will. I have heard of droms going where a rider did not wish to go at the time—usually the drom took him directly to his final goal. I have never heard of one continuing on when the man he was accompanying stopped."

There was little to relieve the tedium of the ten days it took them to reach the area of shifting sands. Twice they were attacked by silverfish and three times by crabs. Lahks was not amused. For three of them armed with laser, there was not enough danger to be exciting, and destroying the creatures seemed mere butchery. There was, however, no trick either Lahks or Stoat could think of to distract the nearly mindless hunters, and the skins and clear carapaces were loaded into the flyer as trade goods. With each addition to their cargo, Stoat grew more doubtful. That night in the tent he voiced his concern.

"Beldame, we will never get this off-planet," he objected sadly.

"We can try," Lahks insisted. "It will look more reasonable than leaving empty-handed. What we need is a cup large enough for a spacer to land in but well away from an inhabited area. Do you know of such?"

"Yes, but I do not think I would sacrifice one for our escape. They are all the sweet life left on this dying world. My faith says there is no heaven and no hell. All reward and retribution is in this life. I do not believe much, but this I do believe. And I fear the retribution I would suffer—if not from my Nameless God, then from my own conscience—if I destroyed one single drop of life in this ocean of death. Would you call a spacer to burn the little house or the garden it lives in?"

Lahks caught Stoat's hands in hers. "Twice-born, Twice-born, it is plain why you have lived when the others died. How came you to keep so soft a heart, so clear an eye for beauty, in spite of the grinding and winnowing of time?"

A spark of emotion so intense passed between them that both gasped in unison. A moment later they chuckled in chorus, too. This was not the time or place. Shom sat almost knee-to-knee with them, and, more important—because both had experienced societies where lovemaking was a public, rather than a private, act—they were dirty, raw with the rubbing of grit against their unwashed bodies, and too intent on their purpose to give their minds and bodies to an act that required utter totality to make it worthwhile.

Their hands dropped apart and Lahks returned to their problem. "You said that men had tried to live in the cups, but that they turned into desert since the plants and animals did not reproduce fast enough. Are there none..."

Air hissed between Stoat's sharp teeth. "Of course," he interrupted. "I never think of them as cups. They are abominations, deader than the rest of this world because their protection holds well and even the dragons and crabs do not come there. Of course. Now, let me see."

He leaned sideways over an empty spot of floorspace and beat at his chest and arms. A fine layer of dust sifted from his windsuit to the floor. With a wetted fingertip, Stoat began to sketch a map.

"This is Landlord Tanguli's cup, and here is Vogil's; here are the mountains between. It is between seven and ten planet days' walk. That will give you the scale. South, the mountains curve westward. To the East, however, about here, there is a dead cup. I am sure it is large enough."

Lahks sat studying the map. Finally she asked slowly, "What is the stuff in the flyer worth off-world?"

"A fair sum. Some thousands of credits, even unfinished."

"Enough to draw a Trader so far from his accustomed site where there is no chance to sell, as well as to buy?"

"No, but that is less the lack of value than the fact that no Trader would wish to anger the Landlords."

"Then it will have to be the Guild," Lahks said lightly.

Stoat grimaced. "It will be a long wait, even if your call reaches them."

"Not so long, perhaps. I interested them enough to put a Watcher on me and hinted I would have business for them. They know what comes from Wumeera. I have a code frequency."

"Beldame," Stoat said with a twisted smile, "will you tell me what you are? It does not matter, but I am curious. I should hate to die tomorrow not knowing why one who is no Trader has such knowledge of their ways, why half a Changeling should have a code frequency for calling the Guild, where you came by that comcov, which is no product of commerce—and the whys and wherefores of a few other matters that should have no connection with the gently reared Freelady you seem to be."

Lifting her eyes from her continued contemplation of the rough map, Lahks smiled. "I must have forgotten to say that I am a Guardian trainee. It did not seem important after I had told you of my Changeling heritage. That is my secret. My relationship with the Guardians I suppressed only to enhance my freedom of movement."

A deep chuckle shook Stoat. "There is *something* forbidden to the Guardians?" he asked with cynical sarcasm.

Lahks chuckled, too. "Well, no, but we are not deeply beloved, and I did not wish to be distracted from seeking Ghrey by irrelevant attacks."

"Ghrey Mhoss," Stoat muttered, his brows drawing together. "Ghrey Mhoss ... Oh! He who inspired the Kssyssyk rebellion?"

Lahks was again studying the map, but she nodded abstractedly.

"Some hundreds of thousands of men were massacred by the white slugs of Kssyssyk in that rebellion," Stoat said flatly.

"Mmmm," Lahks agreed, nodding again, her lips pursed in

her absorbed contemplation of travel time from the dead cup to Tanguli's cup.

Stoat's hand shot out and gripped her arm. "Why? Was it carelessness, miscalculation, incompetence?"

At that question Lahks looked up, puzzled and very faintly indignant. "Don't be ridiculous. Ghrey is not careless or incompetent, and the Guardians never miscalculate a mission because there is always a long enough time to reconsider and redirect events. Kssyssyk was a great success, planned and worked on for centuries before Ghrey brought the work to fruition." She studied Stoat's tight face for a moment, then shook her head gently. "It was necessary that the people of Kssyssyk should know themselves. Twice-born—you who look back on the ages—look forward now. Those people think in a pattern so different that their scientific treatises and children's textbooks are imported as works of art—sculpture and painting—by many worlds. No method of communication on abstract matters has yet been devised, although in concrete, physical things there is no problem in gaining a common understanding. It is thought that they taste time and smell mass, that they see or hear atomic structure—but no one is sure."

"But so many lives..."

"In your millennia, Twice-born, how many billions have died of age, of sickness, of grief, or of boredom for no purpose at all? The people of Kssyssyk had gone too far into easy, idle life in which thought totally replaced action. For a thousand circles of their sun the Guardians watched the population drop until extinction threatened. We could not understand their books—if books they are—but nothing new touched their technology, social structure, or government. Toward the end, they did not seem able to repair technological artifacts that ceased to function. It was time to rouse them."

"But a whole population of colonists!"

Lahks' eyes twinkled. "First, it was a population of Homo sapiens, of which—as your God and my Power know—there are enough and more than enough of in the universe. Second, if you knew the colonists who were deliberately sent to Kssyssyk, you would have said good riddance. Third, it was not really quite so many who died. Those of Kssyssyk were pacifists, you know. It was necessary to give them some protection, and a reputation for ferocity is helpful." She sobered. "But many did die, on both sides. There was no massacre; it was a war, brutal and bloody, but very nearly fair. The superior numbers and technology of Kssyssyk was balanced by the people's lack of knowledge that many of their devices were marvelous weapons and, worse, their almost hysterical reluctance to use the weapons."

"A whole population is not wiped out in a war," Stoat snarled.

"In fact, it was not, but it would not have mattered if it had been. The Guardians do not protect the weak, nor do they disrupt worlds for some deep and long-laid plan of conquest, nor do they create havoc for amusement. The Guardians guard against stasis. Stasis is the enemy of intelligence, and stasis we battle—with kindness when possible, with blood and cruelty when needful."

"And the Institute, no doubt, is the Nameless God."

"Oh, no." Lahks laughed into Stoat's angry face. "The Institute has been given many names and none of them is nice. Stoat, when I have found out why my father wishes me to come to him, we will go to Kssyssyk and squirm in the burrows with the white, slimy slugs. We will smell their science, taste their houses, and, if you like, visit those of the colonists who still live there."

"Kssyssyk is a closed planet."

"But I am Ghrey Mhoss' daughter and a Guardian trainee. Do not misunderstand me. Kssyssyk happened to be an easy, cheap, sweet operation. It would have made no difference if billions had been slaughtered, so long as there remained sufficient people on Kssyssyk to breed. The intelligence of Kssyssyk was dying out because they thought they were happy as they were, and any means was valid to save it. That is the raison d'être of the Guardians. We do not count cost in lives. We do not care if civilizations crash. We are Guardians only of types of intelligence. The people of Kssyssyk are not happy now. They are barbarians compared with what they were, but they remember greatness. Their technology has been smashed, and they are relearning and rebuilding with infinite pain and sense of loss."

Stoat stared at her. Her face was alight, her eyes burning with enthusiasm, all laughter swallowed up in dedication.

"If they knew the Guardians had engineered their fate, they would hate us, as many do, but already there are signs that it is not *mere* rebuilding. New paths are being taken. Departures from old patterns..."

Suddenly Stoat nodded and interrupted her. "The curse of the immortal is to value individual life above all else. My intelligence tells me you are right. My emotions are revolted by the thought of inciting situations that could bring about death."

Lahks smiled. "Well, if we do not get that flyer over the rolling rocks tomorrow, the conflict will have to remain unresolved. If we do...oh, perhaps we can reeducate your emotions."

Chapter

13

In fact, getting the flyer over the rolling rocks proved to be no feat at all—although it cost Stoat and Lahks both their dignity and their temper.

When the sand began to shift underfoot enough so that they staggered like drunkards and the wind was so strong that at times Lahks was lifted and shaken at the end of her leather tether, Stoat fixed on a rise in the sand that he thought suitable for takeoff. Neither Shom nor Lahks could hear him over the screaming gale, but eventually they made out his pointing arm in the haze of flying sand. Obediently they shifted so that the angle of their pull would make the droms push in that direction. And, promptly, the ship stopped dead.

For some time they did not notice this. The sand was moving; the air was little less solid than the ground underfoot. They pulled earnestly, huffing and puffing, until a slight easing of the wind's pressure drew their attention. There, close on the right, blocking as much of the gale as possible, squatted three large silvery figures, their eyes rolling up and down, dizzily, their heads bobbing joyfully, their white teeth gleaming in idiotic grins.

Even then it took Lahks a while to realize what had happened. Her will was so fixed on getting the flyer up the rise that her mind was locked into her body's effort. At first she felt mildly annoyed that the three additional droms did not help those that were pushing. Slowly it percolated into her brain that the three were squatting. Squatting! Sitting still! The ship was not moving. With a gasp of mingled rage and exhaustion, Lahks stopped pulling and squatted herself.

Stoat's mental processes must have followed an identical path. Within amin, Lahks saw him struggling past Shom, stopping him, inching toward her in the lee of the ship. For one instant they were close enough so that she could see his face through the clear plate. It was distorted by rage; the eyes were narrowed, the lips curled back in a feral snarl.

Lahks understood far too well. They were so close to success, so close. Her own angry despair was kindled by his. Together they staggered and crawled toward the droms. Together they fought them, kicked them, dragged them by the ears. But neither Stoat nor Lahks, for all their rage, was an irresistible force, and the droms certainly approximated immovable objects very well.

Lahks knew she was screaming blasphemies, that tears were pouring down her face and leaking out of her face plate, depriving her of moisture she could ill afford to lose. It was the cheerful acceptance by the droms of their ill-treatment that was driving her over the edge of reason, and when one put out a long pink tongue and licked her with obvious affection, she collapsed, sobbing.

Perhaps that restored Stoat's rationality. The next thing Lahks knew, he was tugging her toward the ship. At first she resisted, but sand had already started to build up against her where she lay and the fear of being buried alive made her crawl forward with him to seek shelter.

Inside they found Shom sitting quietly, cross-legged, staring at his stone. Wearily, Lahks lifted her face plate and wiped her face. Stoat was leaning back against the door breathing in great tearing sobs. After a strained silence, he lifted his face plate, too, and sighed deeply. His lips were thin and hard, his eyes bleak.

"I am sorry, Beldame. I think this must be my fault."

"How can it be?"

He shrugged. "I must wish to die. I am not conscious of it." For a moment a smile lit his eyes as they rested on Lahks. "In truth, for the first time in more years than I care to remember, I only feel a burning desire to live—but they read the id. Shom has no id. You—no, you are life. It must be me."

117

"I doubt it, Twice-born. If you wished to die, we would never have come out of that camp after we first moved the ship."

"Then, why? It must be me." He moved restlessly to touch the controls and then to stare blindly out at the droms. They were barely visible, near the ship but somehow appearing smaller, as if they were shrinking. Stoat's mind squirmed, seeking a loophole, but he was very tired and it seemed impossible to fool a creature that responded to your id. At last he sighed again. He had wanted the relationship with Lahks that seemed to promise for the future. She had sparked something in him that no woman had awakened for centuries.

"I will go out," he began slowly. "One of the droms will follow me, but the others..." His voice checked suddenly and his body stiffened.

Lahks had repressed her instinctive protest, applied her training rather than her emotions to the situation, and was coldly considering her chances of lifting a ship with which she was totally unfamiliar in wind of such velocity. She even pushed the black button to be sure that personal preferences were not influencing her. The decision was, all factors considered, that it would be safer to have Stoat try to raise the ship from an unfavorable site than to make the attempt herself. As she opened her mouth to tell Stoat, his unnatural stillness dawned upon her. She had risen, her hand wavering toward her stunner, when she heard him speak again.

"Damned droms," he muttered. Then he shrieked at the top of his lungs, "Damned droms!" And he launched a furious kick at the nearest object, which happened to be the pilot's seat.

The immediate effect of this outburst of temper was a new string of obscenities, most of them in languages Lahks had never heard, while Stoat hopped around on one foot, holding the other. Lahks now had her stun-gun out. There was no room in the confined cabin for a fit of hysterics, however justifiable. Stoat slid himself into the pilot's seat. Lahks took aim. She could not permit him to take off in a blind rage. He did not reach for the controls, however; he turned to her a face twisted by a weird mixture of pain, anger, frustration, relief, and laughter.

"Wait," he gasped, his voice shaking in the roil of emotions, "wait until we find those who made the droms. If there is one left, I will slaughter that one with my own hands. If none is left, I will devote my eternity to the invention of a time machine so I can go back and kill them all."

Lahks' lips had begun to tremble with incipient giggles. Plainly, something Stoat had seen out the window had wiped away his fears. It was something he felt he himself should have known or guessed ahead of time, which was why he was so angry.

"I gather we are safe," she remarked with unnatural gravity. To yield to the laughter that was shaking her inwardly would merely set Stoat off again, and with his penchant for kicking things... A little gurgle escaped her. Stoat cast a jaundiced eye in her direction. For a moment his passions struggled with one another.

"Damned droms," he gasped, and he laid his head down on the control panel, shouting with laughter.

"But what did they do?" Lahks asked weakly when sobriety returned.

"Figured what I *should* have figured, that by the time we climbed it and were ready to lift off, the rise I selected would be a hollow. I suppose I'm tired. I didn't realize how fast the sand was shifting. In fact"—Stoat peered through the window—"I had better prepare to fire the engines. This bit will reach its peak very soon."

"Figured?" Lahks questioned, having scarcely heard the rest of Stoat's remark. "To be able to 'figure' is to be able to reason. And reason implies intelligence. Stoat..."

"Don't ask me," he said sharply. "I don't know. A computer 'figures,' too, but it has no intelligence."

"A computer follows some kind of program, no matter how vague, and does not read minds or ids or whatever."

"Then let us find those who created the drom and ask them."

"Unless," Lahks said slowly, "the droms are the intelligent life form on this planet and, for some reason of their own, choose to..."

"Let them be," Stoat snapped, flicking switches. "Don't tell me their life-style hasn't changed. There's plenty going on on this planet, and the droms are in it up to their silly eyeballs. It isn't Guardian business." He took a breath, made the cabalistic sign for luck, and pushed the starter.

The flight was tense, but they were never in any danger that

Stoat's skillful piloting did not avert. Lahks was frankly relieved. She knew that several times she could not have saved the flyer. Actually, their troubles began after they had run out of fuel and landed. Stoat made no move to leave the ship but looked anxiously through the windows, checking direction finder and wind gauge repeatedly. Finally he shook his head and turned to Lahks.

"Something is wrong, but, unfortunately, I do not know what it is. If our direction finder is right, we should be out of the belt of violent wind. In that case, we are caught in a storm. But our direction finder may be at fault. I would not be surprised, considering the knocking around this ship has taken. In that case, we may have gone around in circles or be far off our course or simply have traveled a shorter distance than I thought so that we are still in a high-wind area."

Lahks was silent, probing within herself. Then she said surely, "We haven't gone around in circles, and we have been traveling roughly north—but that's all I can tell you. My sense of direction is firm, but vague. In any case," she added, looking out of the window, "we had better get out of here. The sand is building up along the ship."

"I know," Stoat replied softly. "That's why I said we were in trouble—and yet we are lucky, too. If the ship had been on skis, we would have been overturned and rolled around. Eventually the sand would have worn through the ship plate. As low as we are, the sand will cover us. There is the possibility we could dig out after the storm—if this is a storm—but it would be impossible to live outside the shelter of the ship. Even if we could get the tent up—and I doubt we could or that it would stand up to a storm—it would be buried, too. We are safer here, where we have some oxygen."

"I don't like the idea of being buried," Lahks said uneasily.

Stoat laughed without mirth. "I don't like it, either." He listened to the wind and the rasp of the sand on the metal of the ship. "I do not know whether we could walk in that wind as it is, but I do know that if it got any worse it would first rip off our suits and then our flesh. That's a hell of a way to die. We are too tired to go far." He shrugged fatalistically.

Lahks looked through the window again, but it was darkening so rapidly that she could not see the insidious rise of the sand along the ship. Silently she got out food packets and, a few amin later, a torch. Ghrey had certainly been right. The heartstones were not dangerous, but Wumeera was a planet to be treated with the greatest caution. Lahks was aware by the time they had finished eating that the sound of the wind and the hiss of the sand were much diminished. The windows were now pitch-black, utterly unrevealing, and she glanced toward Stoat. He was very busy adjusting the position of a small oxygen cylinder and attaching a valve to it—much too busy to catch her eye.

She stood quietly, wondering whether she wanted to know the answer to the question in her mind, then said uncertainly, "Stoat?"

His hands became totally still for an instant and his eyes did not lift to hers. Then he said. "Shom, go sleep in the pilot's seat." And when the big man had settled himself, Stoat reached back and unfolded a silverfish skin so that it made a rug. Finally he turned toward Lahks, his hand at the closure of his windsuit.

It was enough of an answer. He was offering her all the comfort he had to give—the warmth of his body. Lifting the headband of her face plate and throwing back her hood, Lahks moved toward him.

Chapter

14

Morning did not dawn; it rose like thunder. At least that was the impression that Lahks had of the sound that woke her. She turned slightly in Stoat's arms and heard him mutter, "Damned droms."

Since opening her eyes had brought no light, Lahks fumbled for the torch and flicked it on. Stoat grinned wickedly, his sharp teeth glittering through thin lips. "We were buried, I guess, but we're being saved," he remarked. "Only I wish the rescue squad didn't get up so early."

"Did you know they would come?" Lahks asked, laughing.

"I hoped without conviction," he answered. "I heard of a man who had been dug out after a storm." He glanced quickly at her and smiled. "I did not wish to raise false hopes. It was better to be prepared to dig out ourselves." He broke off to listen to the sounds and then burst out, "Damn those droms, we'll have to dig out, anyway. Those idiots are trying to get to us through the roof."

While he spoke, Stoat was sliding into his stillsuit and windsuit in sinuous movements that awoke Lahks' memory. She grinned and hurriedly put on her own garments. She had been too busy and then too tired to worry about being buried alive last night. Shom was now awake, too, and struggling with the door. Sand had been forced into the track and was keeping it from sliding.

Suddenly the growl of moving sand and rock was replaced by the screech of metal on metal. "They are not only trying to get in through the roof!" Lahks exclaimed, staring at a long dent that had appeared. "They are going to succeed! What are their claws made of?"

"The Power that Is doubtless knows—and their makers, but no one else. Men have taken everything else on this planet apart and analyzed it, but droms are invulnerable."

"Look!" Lahks cried and moved to shelter near the wall.

A slit was now open in the metal and this was being widened rapidly into a tear. Almost immediately a drom's silly head, eyes bobbing back and forth between the double lenses, poked through. Lahks and Stoat sighed resignedly in chorus. If the droms had decided they were to come out through the roof, they knew no way of changing that decision. The head was withdrawn. The rent widened quickly.

Half an hour later the silverfish hides and crab carapaces were loaded on the droms. Lasers loose in their holsters and packs on their backs, the three set out for the dead cup. One thing weighed heavily on Stoat's mind and, for his sake, on Lahks'. It was obvious that all three of them could not appear at Tanguli's cup. Whatever the relations between the Landlords, there was no question that all of them would look without favor on robbery and mayhem. The loss of a flyer on a world where all mechanical objects had to be imported was a major catastrophe. Tanguli would turn them over to Vogil as soon as they were recognized.

Of course, to avoid recognition was no problem at all for Lahks. She could change her coloring, her size, and her sex. Stoat was an ordinary-enough-looking man. A touch of gray in his hair, pads in his cheeks and lips, a more yellow cast to his dark skin, and no one would give him a second glance. Shom was the problem. Even if it had been possible to conceal his blue-eyed fairness and the massive size that would mark him in a world of small, dark people, his mental condition would have betrayed him. It was impossible to teach him to act a part, equally impossible to believe there would be two men in his condition wandering the deserts as hunters.

Shom must be left behind. There was agreement on that subject and even on the method to be used. Shom would not suffer. Lahks would drug him into stasis. Unfortunately, the equipment that ordinarily was used to keep the stasis-drugged alive indefinitely was lacking. For about ten days the only effect of the drug would be beneficial. Shom would react as if he had ten hours of healthy sleep. After that, degeneration would start. Death would supervene in about a month.

Stoat told himself that it would be no tragedy. In many ways, Shom had long been dead. But at least he had had some pleasures, and since he had been given the stone he had been truly and deeply happy.

The very night they arrived at the dead cup, Stoat adjusted the almech and said to Shom, "We have to bury the trade goods. Dig."

By morning the space was wide enough and deep enough. The skins and clear carapaces were carefully piled together and covered with the dead earth of the cup. On one edge there was a hollow, padded by the slick silverfish hides, still uncovered. Shom stood at one end of this, lifting the almech, which would throw a stream of earth over the cache.

"Shom," Lahks said compellingly.

He looked up, and she reached out and touched his throat not far from the angle of the jaw where the lifted face plate left the skin bare. There was just time for Stoat to catch him and ease him down. In the lurid red light—the light of late evening that was the best the dying sun of this dying planet could provide, even at morning—Stoat turned the stream of earth from the almech on the still form of his companion.

Lahks had lowered the face plate, composed Shom's limbs so that they would not be bruised, slipped the breathing tube under the face plate, and covered all with another silverfish hide. She turned to comment on the neatness of the operation, but the words died in her throat. All intensity had gone from Stoat. His expression, his eyes, were as dead as the dust he was piling on his companion.

"He isn't dead," she offered experimentally.

Empty eyes, the feral flicker gone from them, met hers. "Do you know how many I have cast earth upon? Hundreds? Thousands? Long before you were born I lost count. I swore I would not, ever again...."

The hole was full. Stoat checked to be sure it was not filled too evenly, readjusted the almech, then sprayed earth smoothly. Lahks watched. Certainly his efficiency was not impaired by the emotional shock—not grief. Stoat was not grieving over Shom—no one could; he was merely responding anew to a multiple memory of grief too often endured and overcome.

Lahks touched the black button. Coldness flowed in. The pure calculating mind—free of sympathy, empathy, all emotion—considered. It was unfortunate that there were too many variables—as was usually the case with single-entity behavior. For mass-entity situations, most variables canceled out, and the behavior of a population could be predetermined. It was funny—Lahks did not smile because she was incapable of smiling with the black button down. Funny, a good word comprising both odd and humorous, another section of the detached mind judged—that for single entities the reason-emotion response of the indweller's body (the mind when free referred to itself as the indweller, to Lahks as a whole as the indweller's body) was as adequate as the pure reason of the indweller. Conclusion: relinquish control to the indweller's body. Lahks lifted her mental finger. Warmth lit her eyes as she watched Stoat methodically redistributing the necessary supplies into two packs. She did not rush him, but she was filled with a sense of urgency. If they could return in time and resurrect Shom undamaged, that act might be the key that could lock the door on Stoat's past—on the lives he had lived while others, loved and unloved, even whole nations, had died and had earth cast over them.

"Do you think there is any part of you—ego, id, or superego—that doesn't want to get to the radio in Tanguli's cup?" Lahks asked as she shrugged into the pack Stoat handed her.

He stood for a moment considering her implication. The tense wariness was already coming back into his eyes, making his expression alive. "Ride the droms," he mused, pursuing her thought, rather than her words. "We would save two days." He paused a moment, looking at the waiting creatures, wondering briefly where the third had disappeared to, then nodded. "Yes. Let's ride the droms."

They saved more than two days. Apparently they had

underestimated their desire to arrive. The droms did not stop at all. Day and night, outrunning the silverfish, avoiding the crabs, outclimbing the dragons through the mountain range, the droms drove onward. Travel in a flyer was swifter, but not much more comfortable. Nodding off to sleep, Lahks found that the backrest the drom provided curved around to grip her firmly so that she could not fall off. Only when they crossed a flat and the impact of the wind-driven sand seemed about to rip her windsuit from her body did Lahks think of the more sheltered vehicle.

She thought of it again as they crossed the flat leading to Tanguli's cup, and she realized that no attempt had been made at disguise. Had they stopped for the night or been in a flyer, Lahks could have worked on Stoat. As it was, she dared not even raise her face plate to call to him. For herself there was no problem. She thought of—and became—a native youth. And she told herself she need not be concerned about Stoat. He had not survived millennia without facing similar situations.

What did concern her was that it soon became apparent the droms would take them directly to Tanguli's manor. At that, she had again underestimated either the force of their desire to get at the radio or the warped sense of humor of the droms. When the guard opened the gates of Tanguli's manor, the creatures stormed right past him, right between the domes, until they came to the side of the Landlord's own building. Here they stopped, but only to begin tearing at the stone with their invulnerable claws.

The guard had lifted his stunner as they passed, but he had no chance to fire. Shouting a warning, he ran full-tilt up the street after the invaders. When he saw what was happening, his eyes bulged, but he was a well-trained young man. Without attempting to find out why two droms, who had never come into an enclosure within anyone's memory, should dash in and try to tear down the Landlord's home, he fired.

As Lahks and Stoat sagged limply into the projections the droms had extended to keep them from falling, the creatures stopped tearing away the wall and squatted peaceably. They made no objection to the guard and several others, who had rushed up to help, removing Lahks and Stoat from their backs, and, free of their burdens, they rose and ambled gently away. A replacement guard at the gate opened it for them in a somewhat bemused manner. He watched, but he dared not leave his post, so he could not tell what they did after rounding the bulge of the outer wall.

Meanwhile, Lahks and Stoat had been conveyed to carefully separated cells, stripped, and dropped unceremoniously on stone extensions that served as bunks. Recovery should have taken four to eight tu, but bodies that had learned to regenerate, even to change their basic structure, made nothing of absorbing and repairing the damage done by a stunner. Lahks was fully conscious before they had finished stripping her. Even so, she lay limp, an arm and leg twisted uncomfortably for a long time before she slitted her eyes open a hair. She knew there was no person near enough to watch her because there was no breathing, but she could not tell about electronic watchers.

Finally, in a series of small convulsive shudders, which might be taken as nervous twitching, she managed to switch on her interior scanning network.

The cell was clean. Lahks opened her eyes to make sure there were no mirrors or other spying devices and then sat up, giggling softly. All that effort to turn on her electronic equipment when she could have put out a pseudopod. . . . She did so now, making a cute little tentacle that turned off the scanners. It was nice to be a Changeling, Lahks thought warmly.

Now to find Stoat. The cell was very efficient. It was well lit by many clear plates set in the stone outer wall. The three inner walls were solid stone, except for the door. This had a grid window that a guard could look through and a small opening at floor level through which a food bowl and cup could be passed.

Lahks considered the grille and shuddered. In spite of what the heartstone had taught her, she did not fancy the notion of turning herself into a mass of separate strands like a bowl of spaghetti. She was not at all sure she would ever get the strands back together again. One long string was also impractical. It would take too long to ooze through the grille.

She touched the lock of the cell door. Her fingers thinned, extended into flexible rods, then retracted. As she had thought, there was a mechanical alarm attached to the lock. If the key was not left in it when the door was opened, it would betray tampering. Since Lahks was as naked as the day she was born and the cell was so empty it was dust-free, there was nothing with which to jam the alarm.

Well, there was the slot at the bottom of the door. If it was not ideal, it was better than the other possibilities. Lahks promptly became a rather oddly shaped snake and worked her way painfully out of the slot. In the corridor she lay still, gasping with effort. Her respect and admiration for the limbless reptiles had increased enormously. It was incredibly difficult to move by flexing muscles in your belly. Then she chuckled softly. It was, she supposed, like the old story about foreign children and how clever they were to be able to speak a foreign language so well so young.

For convenience Lahks added legs to the snake's body. It needed ten pairs, but then moved quite swiftly and silently. She stuck her flattened and elongated human head through the slot of the next cell. It was empty, as were the second and third in the row. The fourth was at the corner. By now Lahks was sufficiently absorbed in her search that she did not hear the soft footsteps in the cross corridor. As she stuck her head into the slot, two shrieks rang out simultaneously.

Inside the cell, a man screamed, "I'm cured! I'm cured! I'll never touch another drop!"

Outside there was a ululation of pure terror and a young voice yelled, "Monster! Monster!"

Lahks drew out her head, threw her long body upright against the wall, flattened still further, and made like a row of stones. Footsteps pounded as a guard tore down the corridor, rounded the corner, and ran up the other side. In a few moments he came back more slowly, peering suspiciously right and left. Lahks could hear sobbing in the cross corridor and the guard's voice reassuring whoever it was that it must have been a trick of the light.

Fortunately, the youngster was so shaken that whatever errand the two had was put aside. They retreated in the direction from which they had come. Lahks, giggling with the irresponsibility that shape-changing bred in her, resumed her convenient, if peculiar, form. She could, of course, have chosen something else, but she had conceived an affection for the weird body shape. She hurried back down the corridor, past her own cell. The next was again not occupied; the second had a prisoner, but he was fortunately asleep; the third was empty, too.

When Lahks' head slid into the fourth cell, her eyes met those of a black man. His mouth opened, as if to scream, the whites showed all around his eyes, and Lahks began hurriedly to ooze backward.

"Lahks!" It was a sharp hiss, and the thick black lips parted to emit Stoat's chuckle. "In the name of my Nameless God," he muttered as Lahks slid the rest of herself into his cell and then regrew her multiple legs, "I don't know whether I should forswear drink or take to it. I think I preferred the snakes on your head. At least I could look at the rest of you."

"Well, I could have been a pretty fancy dancing girl, but I'd like to see one get through that slot."

Stoat glanced at her again, then resolutely turned his back and gazed through one of the clear plates. He could see nothing but a patch of gray stone wall, but that was better than Lahks.

"Maybe it's practical," he admitted, "but it does something to my stomach—on top of that stunner. Do you mind if I don't look?"

"Never mind your stomach," Lahks giggled. "What did you do to the rest of yourself?" I didn't recognize you."

"Pills make my skin dark, and I dehaired my head in that last mountain range. I've got slots in my nose, cheeks, and lips to take plastic pads. Let's get out of here fast, though. The damned pads hurt like hell and the pain-killer I took is wearing off."

"Sorry." Lahks found the flat statement very sobering. "I'll be as quick as I can. I have to send that message to the Guild and I have to spot where the flyer is kept. They got the small heartstone in your belt. That will pay for the flyer we're going to steal. It's also as good an excuse as any for what we were doing. We are hunters. We found what we wanted and came here to get a ship off-planet. I hope we can get released. It will make it easier to steal the flyer without raising an alarm."

"Right, but who are you when you aren't that—whatever it is?"

"A young native guide. Look, quick."

Stoat turned his head to examine a young man so typical of the standard native appearance that he was almost unnoticeable. "Good. You are Thessy, from Landlord Tholangi's manor. I took a kid from there with me on my first hunt. He said he knew the ropes. He didn't. He panicked. He's dead. But they don't know that at Tholangi's, so Tanguli can check on you by radio. I—that is, Stoat—abandoned you [they already know that Stoat is an unprincipled bastard] and I—Kwambu—found you in a live cup and we hunted together. Oh, God!"

The last was wrenched from Stoat as he saw the young native disintegrate into the legged snake. He turned away again.

"They won't come for us for four to eight tu," Lahks said, ignoring Stoat's distaste. "How's the pain?"

"You endure what you must," Stoat replied bleakly.

"How about a boost on that pain-killer? Would it help?"

Because he was in pain and the aftermath of the stunner had muddled his fine perceptions a little, Stoat turned angrily. He did not, at the moment, think Lahks' joke was funny. But the long, flat body was bending toward him, and out of the fourth leg down a delicate, feminine human finger protruded. Stoat made an indescribable noise in his throat.

"Sorry," Lahks said cheerfully. "I know it looks funny, but the stuff's in a needle under my nail, and I wasn't sure just how to use it in this form."

Stoat closed his eyes and offered his arm. "Funny is not exactly the word I would use to describe how you look. I'm an old man," he sighed. "Try not to do things like this to me."

Chapter

15

Lahks' major problem was to get from the cell area to the radio room without being detected. It was all very well to be able to change into any form, but nothing short of invisibility would seem to help in this case. The legged snake would, of course, have to be abandoned. Lahks had not yet seen a domestic animal of any type loose in a dome. Perhaps on such a hard planet pets were too expensive a luxury, but the lack eliminated the possibility of wandering around in that safe disguise. To take human form was simple, but without clothing she would not go unnoticed for long.

Eventually Lahks moved along at random until her ears told her she was approaching a more frequented corridor. Then, at the corner, she made like a stone wall again, but in this case she extruded two pseudopods carrying her eyes. One eye remained in the corridor she was in; the other she extended into the cross corridor. She placed the eyes well above ordinary height because it gave her a better view of the corridors and because she hoped no one would notice them up there.

This maneuver was not completely successful. Although both eyes did see and transmit separate images, Lahks' brain became a little confused about which eye was seeing what image. As a result, when a passerby did come along and Lahks leaped at him, she leaped into the wrong corridor. Fortunately, the man was so stunned at seeing a section of the wall grow two long, clutching human arms and precipitate itself onto the floor of the corridor that he simply stood and stared. This gave Lahks an opportunity to reconnect her eyes, refocus them, and correct her mistake.

Moments later the same man emerged from a storage closet near the cell area and strode somewhat waveringly toward the center of the building. Lahks was aware of a racking duality. On the one hand the constant shape-changing was sending her emotionally higher and higher; on the other hand, she knew intellectually that she might have very little time. The man in the closet would not stir, but if he were on a job, delivering a message, or expected somewhere, his absence would soon be noticed.

That seemed very funny, indeed. Just think of it. They would be looking for him and there were two of him to be found. A rather feminine giggle forced itself from his lips, and another man stuck his head out of a nearby open door.

"Tiensin, is there something wrong?"

"I'm dizzy. I don't feel well," Lahks replied, desperately slurring his/her speech as much as possible in an attempt to disguise the difference in voice and accent. Then, as no one else came to the door, she/he took a chance. "I have to go to the sending room. For the sake of the Powers that Be, head me in the right direction. I'm not sure where I am."

With an exclamation of concern, this new man came out and, seeing Lahks waver on his/her feet, put an arm around him/her. "I'll take you."

They moved off down the corridor, turned left, right, and left again. All the time an expression of deeper and deeper puzzlement was corroding the new man's face, while Lahks, in Tiensin's imitation body, was periodically racked with so violent an urge to laugh that she/he shook convulsively.

"The Landlord sent you with a private message, I suppose," the new man said finally. "Otherwise, I would go for you. Tiensin, something is wrong, very wrong. You are no thinner, yet your body is without substance. You must see the medical at once."

At this, Lahks nearly doubled up. Since Tiensin was at least a third larger than she was herself, her density was necessarily reduced as her volume increased because her mass had to remain constant. She/he was saved from the necessity of reply by an opportune arrival at the sending room. At the door his/her helper stopped in the empty corridor to urge again that Tiensin go to medical at once. Lahks promptly felled him with a neat rabbit punch and stashed him in the nearest storage closet, bound and gagged. Then she/he returned and tapped on the sending room door. When the door was opened, Lahks stepped inside, shrank half a meter, and struck the sending operator behind the ear with carefully controlled force. Ordinarily she preferred not to resort to physical violence because it left aftereffects, but she felt the need to conserve her fingernail supplies of narcotics.

After a little fumbling with the unfamiliar, old-fashioned sending unit, Lahks punched in the code she had been given and the tone identification of the homing device she would set up. Because she had no way to encode any further information, she sent pick-up time—10 sd or any time after that—in clear, hoping that the time period would be meaningless if the other coded material could not be deciphered. Finally, she punched the button for automatic repeat and automatic wipe-out as soon as the sender was shut off.

All that remained to be done was to ensure as long a sending period as possible. Lahks opened the door a cautious crack and peeped into the corridor. No one was coming. A quick reconnaissance permitted her to spot still another storage closet, and soon the sending operator, comfortably but firmly gagged and tied, was reposing in it.

Now for the flyer. Thus far she had been lucky, but increasing and decreasing her size had further elated her spirits. Lahks, keeping a tight rein on herself, determined to take no chances. She waited in the sending room, her eye to a crack in the door. As soon as she saw a man in the corridor, she stepped out and leaned negligently on the wall.

"Tiensin," the new arrival said, "what..."

It was as far as he got. Lahks stepped swiftly forward, touched his throat with one of her little needles, and produced a will-less slave. "Come in here," she said. When the door was safely locked, she added, "If you must speak, speak softly. On this paper draw a diagram of the inside of this dome and show where the Landlord's bedroom is. On this other paper, draw all the domes in the Landlord's manor and show especially where the flyer is kept."

After the sketches were complete, and Lahks was sure she could follow them, she said, "Come with me." And went out, locking the sending room door from the inside by inserting a thinned and elongated finger to touch the mechanism from the outside. Finally, she escorted her fourth victim to still another storage closet. This was necessarily some distance away, the closer ones being already occupied, but since the new victim was walking on his own feet, it made little difference.

Unfortunately, they met one man who asked Tiensin sharply what he was doing there. Sighing a little, Lahks hit him. The fourth victim carried the fifth to where he was bound and incarcerated, then farther along obligingly allowed himself to be stored. I had better not do anything else, Lahks thought as she made her way back toward her cell, or all the Landlord's men will be lying around in closets.

This notion fascinated her in the unstable emotional state she was in. By the time she had reached her cell and turned first into the snake to bring Stoat the plans she had already memorized and then back to a native boy in her own cell, she was giggling fitfully while she calculated whether there would be enough storage closets to house all the men, and, if there were not, what positions would be most comfortable for them for double occupancy. Since Lahks knew neither the number of people in the dome nor the number of closets, the calculation, to say the least, was tentative.

Fortunately, nothing passed except time, and enough of that passed to restore Lahks to relative sanity. She was still in good spirits, but no longer bordering on the irrational. It occurred to her that stability of form was not natural to a Changeling and that it might be both a strain and a depressant. Then it would have been the need for stability of form that had permitted her to be serious enough to become a Guardian trainee. That was important. If she wished to continue a purposeful life, it would be necessary to ration her use of her Changeling ability. But there was another alternative—a life of unending joy and exaultation without sorrow or pain, a life of pure laughter literally without care.

Lahks was very grateful when the sound of steps in the

corridor recalled her to the problems of the present. The choice between two good things is always more agonizing than any other. There was no need, however, to concern herself with that choice now. First it was necessary to stay alive long enough to make it.

A guard in a rather elaborate uniform—the first uniform she had seen on this planet, where windsuits with simple tunics under them seemed to be the sensible rule—looked in. Lahks, as the native boy, was sitting quietly with her head in her hands. He ordered her up and told her she was to be taken to the Landlord.

"Like this?" Lahks inquired.

"Why not? It is a very good way to be," the guard responded.

Lahks' training in sociology supplied the reason for the guard's expression before she could betray her true unfamiliarity with Wumeera's customs. Of course, in a group where women were few and cloistered, men would be bisexual or even exclusively homosexual. Lahks cast a speculative glance at the guard. This might provide an easy path to what she sought. She coyly lowered her eyes but did not move away when the guard's hand brushed her flank. Their arrival at the Landlord's audience room prevented any further intimacies or suggestions, but Lahks was satisfied. The seed was planted.

It was apparent from the relative indifference with which Lahks was questioned that Stoat had already been interviewed. Because it should have been impossible for them to have concocted any story together, the fact that Lahks' answers tallied with Stoat's was proof of innocence in Tanguli's mind. Furthermore, he had their heartstone. Indifferent, since no alarm concerning the missing men had yet reached his ears, the Landlord gave orders that Lahks' and Stoat's gear be returned and they be set free. Suits and packs were tossed on the floor from a side chamber and Stoat himself was propelled from it so ungently that he fell, sprawling.

For a few moments Lahks was fully occupied (as a modest young man should be) in donning stillsuit and windsuit. Then she looked at Stoat and gasped. His face was a mass of bruises and blood, his eyes swollen nearly shut, his lips torn. A rage so violent flooded her that her inbuilt defenses went into action automatically. Her body froze and the ever-ready finger slammed the black button down.

Emotion eliminated, the correct responses to the situation

were easy. Stillness melted into a barely perceptible shrinking away from Stoat and became a movement toward the guard who had brought her in. At first he did not move; however, after Tanguli had growled a warning at Stoat about remembering who was Landlord and who was less than dirt and had left the room, the guard picked up Lahks' pack and handed it to her with a smile.

"Why do you stay with that black man?" he asked her.

"I . . ." Lahks hesitated, cast a coy glance at him under his/her lashes, cast a reluctant glance at Stoat, and shrugged. "He saved my life. He offered me a half stoneshare. It was better to be with him than alone in the wilderness."

The guard put a possessive hand on Lahks' arm. "You know that in this cup and all others the law is that stones belong to the Landlord. He has no stone now. And here you are among your own people. Stay with me."

Lahks moved a trifle closer, his/her face downcast. "I would like to stay, but . . . he did save me, and in his way he was kind to me." He/she hesitated a little longer, glancing up appealingly again. "Could I come back? If I just went with him to the town to see him lodged and tell him I wish to part from him could I come back?"

"Yes," the guard agreed. "That would be best. Come back later."

"When you are free from duty?" Lahks smiled suggestively.

"Yes, indeed," the guard agreed heartily, realizing that if the new boy came back before he was free, one of the other guardsmen might steal the first sip of nectar. "After the eighth tu," he said, preening a little. "Ask for Tangu."

Meanwhile Stoat had climbed slowly and painfully into his suit. He was obviously in pain and had to kneel to get his pack on his back. Lahks glanced at the guard again, sighed, and went with reluctance to help Stoat to his feet. Occasionally she had to steady him as they made their way toward the outer gate, but it was only a duty-bound gesture that showed the guard how eager he/she was to be free of this responsibility.

Outside of the manor the two walked in silence until the domes of the town hid them and the droms that followed them from any possible view from the manor. The indweller recognized that no further emergency existed and the black button was released.

"What happened to you?" Lahks cried, pulling Stoat to a crouch and tearing open her pack to get at the aid kit. "Get rid of those pads. Your identity is established. The blackness is enough to carry it."

When he could speak, Stoat sighed, "Sometimes I despair of our species, Beldame. I do not know how old I am—millennia, anyway. I do not know how often in those thousands of years I have met greed and injustice, but still I have not learned." Then he chuckled. "It started reasonably. I did not think it natural to let him take our heartstone without *any* protest, so I blustered a little. Then when he stated the law, I changed off to whining and that was all right, too. And then"—the smile on the bloody lips twisted wryly—"he said that since I had committed a crime by finding the stone, it was forfeit without recompense. I am afraid I lost my head and said what I thought."

"Doubtless it was salutory. I doubt that Landlord Tanguli has heard the truth about himself often," Lahks replied as she finished swabbing Stoat's injuries and began to apply plastiskin.

Anger flickered in the dark eyes. "Salutory for him, but not for us. It gave him an excuse to fine me. He took everything. We have not enough left for a night's lodging in the hotel. Then, of course, I flung away the wisdom of centuries and tried to attack him. I am surprised, really, that they did no worse to me."

"Are you really injured? I saw with what difficulty you moved, but I fell into such a blind rage when I first saw they had hurt you that the indweller took control. Then I could feel nothing and could only act in the way the indweller decided would best resolve the emergency."

"The indweller?" Stoat said uncertainly.

Lahks laughed. "Not a foreign entity. It's hard to explain. Presume that there is a portion of the brain that operates on pure logic, independent of the id and ego. Part of the Guardian training teaches you to separate this portion voluntarily and use it as a computer. Also, any violent emotion triggers an automatic takeover by the computer portion of the brain so that a Guardian cannot act under the stress of overpowering emotion. Never mind that. Are you really hurt?"

"No. After the first kick landed, I recovered my temper. I know how to take a beating. I'm bruised, but nothing is broken."

"Shall I nick you with that pain-killer again?"

"It depends what is next on the schedule."

"The flyer. You heard that invitation to return after the eighth tu. I can convince the guard to take me to the flyer, and I'm pretty sure if it is guarded that I can take care of any guards. I am not quite sure I can master these old-fashioned controls quickly."

Stoat stared past her with unfocused eyes for a moment. "Then never mind the pain-killer. I'll get along. I can't give you a quick course in old flyers, but as I remember the plans you gave me, the flyer is kept near the outer manor wall. If you can drop me a line, I can come over the wall."

Concern leveled Lahks' normally uptilted lips, but she said nothing. Stoat was an adult many hundred times over and knew his own capacity well—when his quick temper was not aroused. She felt around the inner pocket of her superbly fitted stillsuit and, with a smile, extracted a twenty-GC note. Stoat stared, then chuckled.

"I should have known," he muttered, rising to his feet with an effort. His eyes scanned the domes. "I think the hotel is that big one."

With unspoken agreement both began to hurry. Before their eyes danced visions of a fresher, of skin soft, moist, and free of grit, of cleanly scented cloth underclothing comfortably warm instead of the slick clamminess of the stillsuit with its clinging ammoniacal odor. Inured to physical hardship, neither had been conscious of discomfort until relief was imminent.

Although the hotel was neither as neat nor as well run as Fanny's place, they did achieve their main objective of getting clean. Lahks resisted a brief temptation to change back to female form. She would have enjoyed coupling with Stoat again, for he knew more of the fascinating byways of that delight than Lahks had guessed there was to know, but what strength he had left after his mistreatment had to be husbanded. There would be time enough for pleasure when they were off-planet. Sitting cross-legged at the foot of his bed, Lahks concluded a singularly fruitless planning session with a shrug of his/her shoulders.

"There is little that can be decided after all. It depends mostly on whether they found the men in the closets," she commented with a final giggle.

When he/she returned to the manor, it was apparent that they had. There were guards everywhere, mostly in pairs, which increased the difficulty of disposing of them. Lahks considered and then, when she saw where they were heading, made a decision that gave her an unholy glee. She believed very firmly in poetic justice. As she and the guard Tangu, who had been waiting anxiously at the gate for her, neared the Landlord's dome, Lahks hung back.

"I did not know your quarters were in there," he/she said a little breathlessly.

"It will be all right," Tangu replied. "You need not see the Landlord."

"I am not afraid of the Landlord," Lahks remarked with youthful bravado, "but . . ." He/she shrank back again, shaking his/her head, the bravado fading into a rather childish uncertainty. "I am sorry. I cannot go in there. I saw . . ." He/she stopped, swallowed hard, then went on in a whisper. "Perhaps it was the effect of the stunner, but I saw . . . a monster."

Tangu, who had been tugging her along gently, stopped dead. "What kind of monster?"

Lahks swallowed again and shook his/her head. "You will not believe me. I know it was caused by the stunning, but I . . . they looked so real. Only," he/she shrank again against Tangu's side, "I cannot go into that dome. I thought I would be over it, but I cannot go in."

"What kind of monster? Describe it," Tangu insisted.

"There were two," Lahks replied in a small, hurried voice. "One was a long, long flat snake with lots of little legs and—I swear it—a flat, human face. The other—the other was a wall with long human arms and eyes on long stalks." He/she uttered a shaken laugh and added, "You see how ridiculous it is. Such things cannot be."

But Tangu was staring at her with starting eyes. "Where did you see this?"

"Through the grille of my cell. I was so frightened that I could not make a sound. Perhaps I fainted. The next thing I knew, I was back on the bench again. Then I sat up and hid my eyes—and then you came. After that"—Lahks flicked a small suggestive smile—"I was not afraid anymore."

The smile had been insurance, but Tangu did not respond to it. Instead, he gripped Lahks firmly by the forearm and dragged her along. "You must overcome your fear," he said harshly. "This tale must be told directly to the Landlord."

Lahks hung back and protested feebly, the shudders of

suppressed laughter lending verisimilitude to her pretended fear. Very soon, however, she found herself in the Landlord's presence. She was just planning a method for ridding the room of the extraneous guards and councillors when Tangu, ordering her harshly to stand where he left her, made his way toward the dais. After suitable elaborate preliminaries, which made Lahks' opinion of Landlord Tanguli even lower, he gained his master's ear. A spate of whispering on Tangu's part, interspersed with increasingly loud cries of "What!" on Tanguli's part, ended in achieving Lahks' objective for her. The room was cleared and she was summoned to the dais.

Ordered to tell her story again, Lahks did so with greater confidence, with sweeping gestures, one of which touched the Landlord's hand. She went into elaborate detail about the monsters, about their invincibility and their sly ways.

"And," she concluded, "this horror has befallen your manor because you are an evil man, Landlord Tanguli. This coming has been a warning. If you do not mend your ways, if you continue to punish your men for your evil doing, if you continue to rob hunters and take away their heartstones without giving them some reasonable payment, the beasts will return. Each time you do an evil or an unjust act, the beasts will tear at you while you sleep."

Tangu had listened to this with eyes starting with horror. In fact, he was less afraid of the monsters than of what his Landlord would do to him for bringing this madman into his presence. The Landlord did nothing, however, except to stare at Lahks like a fascinated rabbit, and he/she turned to Tangu.

"Well, I've done my best for you. Old Tanguli is going to be very annoyed when he wakes up and finds out he has returned all the money he stole and has donated his flyer to a good cause. I hope the hypnotic suggestion controls him, but if he gets too outrageous, I would recommend assassination. Of course..."

The paralysis of amazement that had held Tangu broke suddenly, and he leaped forward. Lahks, however, was not there. She had stepped aside and shrunk a full meter. The blow that put Tangu to sleep was delivered by a hand the weight and consistency of steel driven by muscles like a pile-driver. Returning to normal size, she felt Tangu's jaw tenderly to be sure she had not broken it.

"You will not remember this," she said to the Landlord. "You will only remember that Tangu was very brave and tried to save you from the fruit of your own folly. Now you will take from your strongbox the sum of money you fined the black hunter this afternoon and give it to me. Then we will go to your flyer. You will order it to be fully fueled and have extra fuel put aboard. You and I will get into the flyer, as if to see if all is ready, and you will move the flyer out of its housing and take off suddenly, go over the wall, and land on the other side."

Chapter

16

It was a beautiful plan, and it would have saved Stoat the effort of climbing over the wall. The only trouble with it was that it did not work. When Lahks and the Landlord were inside the flyer, Tanguli sat and stared at the controls. Lahks had a momentary qualm, wondering whether her supply of hypnotics was faulty or inadequate. Maintaining her calm, she reiterated her instructions firmly.

"Move the flyer out of its housing. Raise the flyer and set it down on the other side of the wall."

Tanguli sat at the control panel, blank and impervious.

Frowning, Lahks asked, "How do you raise the flyer?"

"I do not know," Tanguli replied.

For a moment Lahks stared as blankly as the Landlord. It had never occurred to her that he might not know how to run the machine. Where she came from, everyone could handle a flyer, except perhaps the very old and very young. Smothering a chuckle at her own stupidity, she glanced at the controls, but they were even more old-fashioned than those of Landlord Vogil's flyer. She hoped Stoat could handle them; she could not, at least not without briefing and practice. All in all, there was nothing to chuckle about. She could not use Tanguli to send the guards away because his wooden manner had already made them suspicious. But if he called them . . . Lahks gave the order.

The Landlord stuck his head out of the flyer and called. The guard trotted over. A few moments later the guard appeared to come out. He wore a sour expression and walked over to his companion.

"The Landlord wants to give you special instructions."

That guard disappeared.

After waiting a few moments, the first guard walked back to the flyer. He seemed startled. "Here!" he called to the guards at the wall in a soft, half-strangled voice. "Help!"

Both came running. The first was dropped by a stunner blast from the inside of the flyer, the second by a well-placed chop delivered by the first guard. He now made a quick search of the building and came up with a coil of rope. One end of this he threw over the wall. He was looking about for something to fasten the rope to when it jerked in his hands. Inexorably, his somewhat insubstantial form began to rise as Stoat's greater weight came full on the rope. A litany of blasphemies curdled the night air.

Desperately, the guard shed his shoes. His feet narrowed, hardened, and formed spike-like points. Clinging to the rope, he leaped into the air and came down at the base of the wall, spike feet first. The spikes sank well into the earth. Now the rope tightened again. The guard's clothing hung baggily as Lahks shrank and strained to hold the rope. More blasphemies oozed from her lips as she felt the spikes give. Then, just as it seemed they would slip completely, she heard Stoat gasping softly at the top of the wall. He twisted lithely and slid expertly down—right on Lahks' head. Both collapsed.

"Why the hell didn't you get out of the way?" Stoat whispered incredulously as he rolled off her.

At first Lahks could not reply. She pointed to her feet, still sunk into the earth. She could see the whites of Stoat's eyes travel from her spike feet to her face and then make another round trip. It was all she could see because brown irises and black face were alike swallowed up in the dark.

There was a short period of stunned silence before Stoat asked in a somewhat strangled voice, "That was easier than tying the rope to something?"

"To what?" Lahks asked between giggles. "You didn't give me a chance to look. You grabbed it as soon as it went over."

"One ties the rope first," Stoat said gently, "then one throws it over." There was, however, a suspicious tremor in his own voice, and he rose suddenly and began to walk toward the flyer housing.

Lahks had still not freed her feet because she was laughing so hard, and she hissed after him, "Wait. Tanguli's in the flyer, and he's primed to stun anyone who sticks his head in." She got up. "We'll have to stun him through the flyer in order to get in."

Stoat stopped and looked at her. "What is the Landlord doing in the flyer?"

"I had a lovely plan to save you the trouble of climbing the wall... a lovely plan."

"So why did I end up climbing the wall, anyway?"

"Because that idiot Tanguli never learned to fly his own flyer."

Again there was a brief silence. Stoat seemed to struggle with himself. "Very few Landlords fly their own ships. Very few kings drive their own land cars, for that matter."

"Very few Guardians fight their own wars—but they know how," Lahks replied tartly. "I knew he would not be an experienced pilot, but all he had to do was to raise it, get it over the wall, and set it down."

They had reached the flyer housing, slinking cautiously in the shadows of the wall. In the brightly lit building, Stoat dropped to the ground with a grimace of pain. He used the guard's gun that Lahks handed him to dispose of the Landlord and then swung himself into the flyer. He stood looking at the five bodies cluttering up the floor with distaste. "Do you want this collection for anything?" he asked.

Having freed themselves of the plethora of bodies, Stoat studied the flyer controls and raised his brows. He seemed about to speak, but then snapped his fingers and dropped out of the flyer to kneel beside the Landlord. Lahks, seeing him turn out the Landlord's pockets, leaned out to call softly that she had retrieved their money. Stoat shook his head without replying, but a moment later he extracted a ring with a flat, notched metal device attached. He sighed with relief as he hoisted himself somewhat wearily back into the flyer.

"This ship is so old, it takes a key to make it work," he remarked in explanation. "It's lucky you did bring the Landlord along. It would have taken me an hour to figure out how to start the ship without it."

The key seemed to solve Stoat's problems, however. He had the machine safely out and away in only a little while. Lahks looked out at the stars. So much had happened that it seemed later than it actually was. In reality they had almost a full night ahead of them.

"Stoat," she said suddenly, "let's pick up Fanny."

"You feel that things have been too dull and uncomplicated up till now, I guess." Stoat remarked blandly. "And, no doubt you are sure we will be *persona grata* in Landlord Vogil's cup."

"Well, no, not the latter," Lahks replied with a grin, "but I promised myself I would get Fanny a new stone, and he wouldn't keep it a day if he stayed on Wumeera. Ergo, let him come with us. Besides, I have a soft spot for gorls, and in addition to that, if we have to deal with the Guild he may be useful."

The ship had already begun to swing northeast, but Stoat's head snapped around toward his companion. "Now, wait. Now, just you wait." His voice rose a little. "What is this 'Deal with the Guild' bit? I am not overanxious, Beldame, to get involved with the Guild. Their net stretches wide and . . . I am not unknown to them."

"Retinal pattern?"

Stoat's lips tightened. Then he shrugged and laughed. "Palm prints, fingerprints, footprints, ear shape, retinal and genetic patterns—they have them all."

Lahks emitted a long, low whistle of admiration. "So you were a Master of the Guild. Well, well. You left that pursuit because you felt it to be dull?"

"No, it was interesting enough, but even a Master lives only so long. I left long enough ago to make it dangerous to be recognized, but not long enough ago, I fear, to have the patterns deadfiled."

"I see. You counted on their ignoring you as my assistant. But if we cross them, no one would be ignored."

"Too true, Beldame."

"I won't if I don't have to," Lahks said ingenuously. She watched the cocking of her companion's mobile eyebrows and the wry twisting of his lips. His disbelief in the innocence of her intentions was so patent that she chuckled. "No, really, if they deal Guildwise with us, I will be content. It seems to me, however, that even the Guild would have little control of members working such an outlying planet as Wumeera."

The probability of truth in that statement drew Stoat's brows together in a frown. In its own warped way that is, by its own rules the Guild was honest enough with its clients. It was true that loosely controlled peripheral operators might not abide by the rules when clients themselves, rather than goods that needed to be fenced, were in their hands. In fact, now that he thought back, Stoat remembered he had been instrumental in the chase, capture, and elimination of several such "dishonest" operators. Only at that time he had been a Master, had a dedicated army at his beck and call, and had been doing his "duty" to his organization rather than affronting it. Even with all that going for him, the entrapment and punishment of the malefactors— remarkably mobile malefactors, since they had a spaceship at their command—had not been easy. A glow of amusement lightened his expression.

"You and I and Shom, who is useless in a fight against men, and Fanny are to take on a whole shipload of Guild members very likely pirates—just like that?"

"It will be only a small spaceship," Lahks said cajolingly.

Stoat choked, but before he could reply to her teasing he was forced to give his attention to his piloting. The mountain range that ran between Tanguli's and Vogil's cups was below them, and Tanguli's flyer was so old that it did not have enough lift to rise above the highest peaks. It was necessary to thread through the defiles while keeping a sharp eye on the terrain. Not long after, they set down on the side of the town farthest from the Landlord's manor and Lahks shifted to the form she had used when last here.

"It's too bad we didn't bring the comcov," she remarked.

"I think the flyer will be safe enough. I had no lights and the domes are virtually soundproof. Besides, I have the key. Still, if Fanny cannot be convinced in a short time, we had better take our chances without him. Someone might stumble upon the flyer and report it to the Landlord."

In fact, convincing Fanny raised no problems—as Lahks had foreseen. First of all, gorls were utterly fearless, largely because of their evolutionary history, but also because of their size and appearance. For similar reasons they were not suspicious. Few dared to try to cheat them; those who did were dealt with summarily and ferociously, although with justice. The reputation for tolerating no nonsense added to the generalized reluctance most beings had to infuriate such creatures.

Lahks spoke briefly and to the point, identifying herself and Stoat, offering Fanny a stone, and pointing to the necessity for his leaving the planet. The great head nodded acceptance.

"Price?" Fanny asked.

"You realize that what we are doing is illegal on this planet. We have a caller out for a Guild ship to pick us up at a dead cup. There is a chance they will want our cargo and not want us. We need your help in getting off-planet with our goods, even if it means taking over the ship, killing some of the crew, and bucking the Guild."

The simian eyes stared steadily. "Price reasonable." Fanny grunted at last. "Wait. Get valuables. Let barman keep hotel. Good man. Good worker."

On the way back to the flyer, Stoat remarked to Fanny, "You were easy to convince."

The great fangs glittered briefly in the dim light. "Landlord mad, anyway, for giving rooms. How would know would steal flyer? Unreasonable. Also, only come for stone. Offer stone. Go with. Costs life? Very well. Not living, anyway, running hotel here."

Lahks chuckled. "I had an idea Vogil might be a little annoyed at anyone who had anything to do with us. I'm sorry about the flyer, though. I hope he didn't execute the men who lost it. When we get off-planet, I'll credit him with its worth, or maybe order a new one for him as a nice surprise. Maybe that will cool him off."

Once aloft again, Lahks curled up in the baggage compartment and went to sleep. There were, of course, renegade gorls, as there were renegades of any species, but Fanny did not strike her as the type. Moreover, he had no idea where they were going and could be no danger to them until they had landed and unearthed their cargo. She was a little worried about Stoat. He had been badly mauled by Tanguli's men and had had little rest since then, but there was nothing she could do for him. It was best that she be fresh when they arrived. By then, Stoat would have to sleep.

Fanny showed no suspicion even when they landed in what was apparently an empty cup. Away from the atmosphere of the hotel, he gained in dignity; there was even an air of authority about him as he pushed Stoat back into the flyer.

"Sleep now," he announced. "Trip finished."

"Not yet," Stoat muttered, his black face gray-sheened with the sweat of pain and exhaustion. "We've got to dig Shom out."

"Fanny and I will dig him out, Stoat. You've had it. Go to sleep."

The tight-set lips relaxed, then twitched into a brief, painful smile. "You are so right," he mumbled, and he slid flat and into unconsciousness in the same moment.

Having unearthed the almech from Stoat's pack and located the cache, Lahks proceeded to uncover and revive Shom. Fanny watched in silence, helping when he could. He stared for a moment when Shom's first movement was to open his hand and look at his pea-sized heartstone; in fact, the gorl's body stiffened, but he made no other move or any sound. Lahks and Shom together shifted skins and carapaces, then dug farther until she could remove the hoard of stones.

These she placed into the concave side of a carapace. En masse they were almost too much to look at, but it was en masse that she presented them to Fanny. Again the emotion so inordinately powerful that an alien could read it in his face passed over the gorl.

"I do not know the size of the stone you had, but you may take any one of these."

"Size was that." A finger pointed to a medium, fingernail-sized stone. The pointing hand quivered a moment with longing and then dropped. "Price not paid. Keep stone."

Lahks bowed deeply and sincerely. "Great Prince," she said, "if you do not think it harmful to you, taste your joy. As you trusted me to offer, I have faith that you will pay the price when asked."

"Larger stone maybe make brainsick, but what other harm?"

"I do not know. Do you dream with the stone?"

"Dream?" The gorl stated the word so slowly that he seemed to be tasting it, but at last he shook his head. "Not dream. Desire."

He reached out and picked up one of the medium-sized stones. His head cocked sideways in a surprisingly gay gesture. His whole body seemed to grow lighter and younger. A thick, grumbling wheeze rose from his chest to his lips. "Want to go there"—he pointed outward at the sky—"or there," swinging his hand to another position, "or there. Want to go!"

At first Lahks was afraid that the stone had affected Fanny

badly, but after a few moments the giddiness seemed to pass. He stared at the gently pulsing stone, rubbed it between his hands to increase the pulsations, and stared some more. Finally he hunkered down and faced Lahks soberly. She could see him marshaling his limited Basic to explain something.

"Gorls timid, not about body, but need other gorls. Called Prince. Am. Not rich, how could afford stone? First had, only felt light, happy. Later restless. Wondered how out-planet people live. Traveled. Saw many good things, many bad. Brought ideas home. Some glad; some angry; but much talk and...and ex...ex...experimentation. New paths to gorls. Then stone stolen."

He had been looking at the ground in front of him and occasionally at the heartstone in his hand. Now he lifted his eyes to Lahks.

"Why want?" He held the stone toward her. "Can go see without stone. Not necessary." His shoulders shook and Lahks was again reminded that gorls, like most humanoids, laughed in much the same way. "So many years in hotel. Thinking someday hunter comes here before Landlord takes stone. Offer good price—any price—get new stone. Have stone now. Now not want or need. Understand—understand stone only excuse, so can do what other gorls do not do."

Now Lahks laughed with him. "Stoat and I found out that it is only a learning device. I suppose it has taught you all it can. You can change your mind if you want to and take the flyer back to Vogil's cup."

Fanny drew himself up with a slight show of indignation. "Not want stone, but made Deal. Keep Deal." The simian eyes twinkled. "Besides, want to buck Guild. Never did that!"

They ate, busied themselves with removing the skins and carapaces from the cache and refilling it with earth, and then slept until Stoat awakened. When he had eaten, a council of war was convened. This resulted in building an igloo just large enough for the four of them to creep into out of the crab carapaces and covering it with layers of the silverfish hides. They hoped that from the air the excessive height would not be apparent and that their hideaway would look like a heap of trade goods. The tent was set up near, but not too near, the igloo.

If the Guild landing craft grounded and the crew emerged with peaceful intentions, they could come out peacefully, too. If

THE SPACE GUARDIAN

an attack was launched either from the ship or by the crew, it would be launched against the tent—they hoped. This would give them at least a chance to defend themselves since, presumably, the Guild would not use against them any weapon powerful enough to destroy the stones. Probably they would confine themselves to the use of a stunner—just in case their clients had hidden their treasure.

Lahks did not doubt that they would be able to overcome the landing party. What she and the others could not figure out was how to get aboard the ship. Presumably, when the Guildsmen saw their companions overcome, they would lift the ramp, perhaps even seal the ship. Probably their desire for the stone offered would keep them from taking off altogether. The best Lahks' party could hope for was some kind of trade that would permit them aboard. That, unless they could take the ship over quickly, would be their death warrant.

150

Chapter

17

Ten sd later, Lahks was warned by her personal detectors of the near-space presence of the ship and the group retreated to their igloo. If the tent was sprayed with a stunner from the landing craft, it must have been a direct, narrow-beam hit. They suffered no ill effects in their hideaway. As the ramp came down, Fanny, Lahks, and Stoat removed sections of carapace from their exit places, slithered out, and lay ready in the camouflaged area alongside the pile of hides.

With immense dignity and no hurry, grinning and nodding, four droms marched toward the craft. Lahks heard Stoat's breath hiss; she held her own. If the Guildsmen were familiar with Wumeera, they would know what the droms were—as much as any man living knew—and no harm would be done. If they did not recognize the creatures, they might feel they were being attacked, and then...

The backwash of a stunner blast made Lahks' vision blur and her ears ring. Dimly she heard shouts of consternation. As her eyes focused properly again, she saw a red-violet pencil of light reach from the ship's entrance to the leading drom and break into a coruscating glory of sparks and prismatic displays. Once more, as if their intelligence simply would not accept what their eyes witnessed, the Guildsmen's deadly pencil reached out. More cries of fear and disbelief were uttered as the laser failed to damage the advancing creatures. The droms, without seeming to increase their pace, were devouring the distance that separated them from the ship.

The ramp quivered, began to rise. A sob of frustration shook Lahks. Stoat uttered a low, bitter oath. The leading drom reached the craft. With mincing delicacy it placed its large flat forefeet on the ramp, extended its long neck, as if to peer into the ship, and grinned amiably. The ramp groaned but rose no farther. The second drom had also reached the ship. This one turned about and, looking over its own shoulder, backed up carefully and sat down on the very end of the ramp. There was a faint thud as ramp and drom returned to the ground. The other two droms, apparently beaming with pleasure, squatted to either side of the ramp and nodded vigorous approval.

Lahks was shaking with silent mirth. She did not dare permit her eyes to meet Stoat's for fear she would whoop aloud.

"What are doing?" Fanny asked in a stunned, disbelieving whisper.

"Damned droms! Damned droms!" Stoat muttered, sounding slightly hysterical.

He was, however, controlled enough to recognize the craft. It was old-fashioned, as was natural for such a peripheral area, and lacking in certain refinements. Although it had comcov detects, to either side of the ramp there was an area blind to the ship's sensors, and, therefore, not covered by the ship's weapons. Under normal circumstances the blind spots were easily protected by the men on board, but, with the droms blocking both the view and the line of fire, it might be safe to approach. The danger was in the distance between the igloo and the blind spot, but the attention of the crew was probably centered on the droms.

A few whispered phrases settled the plan of action. Shom was put to sleep with a mild narcotic that could be counteracted in seconds. Stoat and Fanny wiggled to the best position they could and made a dash for the sides while Lahks, to further distract attention, approached the front openly, her hood thrown back to show her features clearly and her streaming hair. To mark herself as a female was multiply valuable. Many humanoid groups still protected their breeders and therefore regarded females as weak. In general, even those cultures that marked no difference between male and female sociologically assumed that humanoid females would be physically smaller and probably weaker. There was, then, less threat to the crew in Lahks' approach and less chance of their attacking without cause.

Whether for these reasons or because there had never been any intention of using force on the ground when it was so simple and untraceable a matter to expel unwanted passengers from an air lock, Lahks reached the area in which the droms were squatting without incident. She passed between the two that were sitting to each side of the ramp and then, moved by an irresistible impulse, stretched up and planted a loud kiss on the snout of the drom whose rump anchored the ramp to the ground.

This mark of affection was accepted with the identical idiotic amiability that had greeted kicks and blows. A tiny spurt of disappointment flickered through Lahks, but she had no time to indulge it.

"Guildsmen," she called, "I am Tamar Shomra. I have trade goods—and something else—to barter for passage and profit. Where is your Cargomaster?"

"Here," a voice replied from inside, beside the opening. "Drive away the beasts, and I will come out so that we can Deal."

Lahks laughed. "If your laser would not drive them away, do you think my great strength will? They do as they like. They are the blessing and the curse of this land," she said, continuing without a tremor of consideration for the truth, "for they are the peace-keepers. Have you ever heard of a war on Wumeera? There never has been one. [This happened to be true because of the low population and because war was almost as difficult logistically on Wumeera as between solar systems.] The droms are opposed to violence. Do not misunderstand me. They are only beasts—I think. But to see violence awakens in them such rage that they destroy everything. As long as we do not come to blows, they are as harmless as kittens and useful, too. They will carry the goods, if need be."

By now, Lahks had sidled around the great rump and was standing directly under the snout of the drom whose forelegs were on the ramp. Cautiously the Cargomaster appeared in the opening.

"We have cargo robots, but we cannot get them out if this *thing* sits in the way."

"I am sorry, Cargomaster," Lahks said. "I can offer you no suggestion." Her voice quivered with memory. "I have on occasion tried to move a drom." She choked. "I was not successful. I give you leave to try, however. They do not mind if you attack them, only if you offer violence to another of your own kind."

The man sidled cautiously forward. The drom turned its head to look at him but only nodded, its eyes bobbing up and down wildly, and grinned. He took another step. "You are alone, Freelady?"

"Oh, no. My companions are to either side of your ship and are well armed"—she laughed aloud—"although I do not know what good that will do us or what harm it can do you. We cannot do anything while the droms are here any more than you can. Come, Cargomaster, and look at our goods."

"And what good will that do," he asked peevishly, "if I cannot load them?"

Nevertheless, he came out, jumping down from the ramp to avoid passing under the drom's head, with its fang-exposing grin, and walked with Lahks toward the cache. He started nervously as the two squatting droms rose and followed.

"They are following us. What do they want?"

"Who knows? They always follow." Lahks paused, as if for thought, then said, "If we load some goods on these, perhaps the others will come to be loaded also. Or perhaps you could push the one sitting on the ramp off with a cargo robot."

Considering that, the Cargomaster stepped out more briskly. He examined the hides and carapaces with cautious approval, going so far as to nod and say, "Prime and unused. There is a market. But that"—his eyes narrowed—"is not what brought us here, Freelady."

Lahks smiled sweetly. "That I have also. And when you are patched in to Guild Central, I will bring it from where it is laid away safely so that we may all agree on price."

By necessity a Cargomaster had total mastery of his expression, and he must have known from the moment Lahks said her companions were in the ship's blind spots that she was suspicious. He shrugged. If she thought Guild Central could protect her... A gasp was drawn from him as a hard snout nudged him from behind. Could the creatures guess?

"They want to be loaded," Lahks said, but the Cargomaster thought the smile she turned on him was sly. Nonetheless, he kept his mind carefully blank and only a trifle reluctantly began to load skins and carapaces onto a flat area on the drom's back that he had not previously noticed.

The drom sitting on the ramp rose and walked away as the loaded ones approached, although the one with its forefeet on the ramp did not move. It continued to crane its neck toward the ship with a curiosity more characteristic of the anthropoids than of the reptilia. For a little while Lahks had thought the droms would enter the ship, but they merely squatted to either side of the ramp as they had before, permitting the skins and carapaces to slide to the ground.

Now a cargo robot trundled out. Lahks made haste to explain that Shom was under the trade goods. "He is brainsick from the stone," she explained glibly. "It was necessary to drug him to keep him quiet." The Guildsman looked at her, his eyes so totally devoid of meaning that she added hastily, "He is dear to all of us and not dangerous. We will have him treated when we reach a civilized planet."

So Shom was loaded tenderly and trundled in with the goods. The Cargomaster gestured politely for Lahks to precede him, but she smiled and shook her head, and Stoat and Fanny, pressed tight along the side of the ship, sidled toward them. Inside they relaxed. Most of their precautions had been in vain. There was no crew, only one young Guildsman directing the cargo robots. They were not too worried about the Cargomaster alone. He did not yet have the stone and he would do nothing until he saw the easiest way to obtain it. In fact, it soon became apparent that they had another lever.

When the Cargomaster saw Fanny, his lips tightened. "A gorl!" he exclaimed.

Lahks smiled demurely. "Prince and Clanmaster Fanny," she offered, bowing her head a trifle in respect.

"People remember favor—even well paid," Fanny said.

In spite of his habit of control, indecision flickered across the Cargomaster's face. Then he turned and headed for the control section of the craft. Their least-favored contingency plan would have to be used. He was not going to harm a gorl Prince and possibly have the Captain slough off the responsibility for that onto him. The original idea had been to relieve the clients of their stone on the landing craft. Then the one crew member who had accompanied him could be killed. His death could be blamed on the clients, all the bodies could be disposed of in space, and the crew as a whole could be kept in ignorance of the prize the Captain and Cargomaster had obtained. Now the crew would have to know about the stone. The elimination of four clients...

His thought checked as a hollow metallic sound and a shriek of surprise from the crewman drew them all back to the hatch. Nodding and grinning, a drom squatted just clear of the ramp closure inside the craft. That the three clients had no part in the drom's behavior was clear. They were open-mouthed, stunned. It must have been his thought about... No, he would not even think it again. But how to get rid of the thing? How? For one irresolute moment the Cargomaster considered using a cargo robot to push the drom out. The notion passed in a flash; he knew no cargo robot could move that mountain of flesh—if it was flesh.

Schooling face and eyes to blankness, the Cargomaster moved again to the com area, with Lahks, Stoat, and Fanny trailing in a rather bemused manner. Lahks woke up enough as soon as connection with the ship was made to stand well within vision range. She did not want anything said between Captain and Cargomaster that would commit them to an action they no longer wished to take. To patch through to Sector headquarters took longer, but no hesitation on the Captain's part gave even a hint of reluctance. Indeed, he was not reluctant. The Guild had improved itself since Stoat's day. Any com sent or received was monitored at Sector so that they already knew about Lahks' party. The Captain had a market for a heartstone and, being from a rim planet himself, felt he could avoid Guild retribution.

It was his very readiness that gave him away. Nonetheless, Lahks made her Deal with Sector, and she bargained hard because she hoped to be able to keep her part of the Deal, whatever the Captain did. The Guild was too useful to Guardians to annoy them more than necessary. Fanny stood beside her, screening Stoat from view with seeming carelessness. When the Deal was closed and recorded, the Cargomaster turned to Lahks.

"And now, Freelady..." In spite of rigid control, his lips

were a little dry and his eyes glittered. "Will you unearth the stone from its hiding place and deliver it?"

Lahks' eyes danced; her lips twitched. She reached into the pocket of her windsuit and drew forth a medium-sized heartstone that responded to handling with a burst of light waves. Rage flickered in the Cargomaster's eyes as he realized she had made a game of him and had been carrying the stone all along. It died as quickly as it rose. He stretched his hand eagerly toward the jewel. The tiny prick he felt, he disregarded for the few heartbeats in which his mind continued to function.

Lahks waited only long enough to be sure the drug had firm hold on him and then turned to Stoat. "Can you take the craft up to the ship, or should we chance his doing it right in this state?"

Stoat checked the controls. They were familiar. "I can, but it makes no difference. They will needle him and us, too, if he walks aboard in this condition. Guildsmen are not backward planet dwellers. If Tanguli's men were suspicious, these will not be deceived for a sec. And what about the crewman back in cargo? And what about that damned drom?"

"Hmmm." Obviously Lahks reconsidered her plan of walking aboard with the Cargomaster as a shield. If Stoat said they would needle down their own Cargomaster, he was sure of it. Lahks turned back to the mind-frozen man.

"When you wake up," she said slowly and clearly, "you will not remember that I gave you instructions or carried the stone with me. This time of waiting will have been spent by my going to take the stone from its hiding place. What you do after you wake up will be your own idea. You will make us your prisoners, bind us and take our weapons, but you will not permit any harm to come to us. You have the stone and you have decided it would be safer, because of the gorl Prince and my connection with Trade, to set us down on some rim planet."

Lahks was sure she would not need to use real brainwashing to inculcate these notions. Probably they were very close to the Cargomaster's own beliefs. She merely was reinforcing those beliefs to turn them into unshakable convictions.

"If we are killed," she continued, "not only will the Guild hunt you, but all the gorls and all Trade will hunt you, too, because the Guild will enlist their aid to punish you. This will raise the odds against your escape too high. If we are left safe, the gorls and Trade will be indifferent. They will feel that your failure to fulfill your contract may be safely left to the Guild to punish. Now, repeat my reasoning."

The little lecture came back word-perfect.

"Good," Lahks said approvingly. "This will sink into your mind, will become a deeply fixed conviction. No argument will be able to shake or change this idea. You will take us prisoner as soon as you wake up, but gently, without violence. We will be too surprised to resist. No one will be hurt in any way. You will accept the drom. It came aboard by itself, but it is valuable. No attempt will be made to expel it from the ship."

"So far, so good," Stoat agreed. "The only trouble is that they'll probably set us down on a primitive, no-call, or interdicted planet. That would give them more time and more freedom."

Lahks shook her head and smiled impishly. "If I cannot get the Captain to agree to a reasonable approximation of the Deal, in other words, as soon as it is clear that they are breaking the Deal so that we will be straight with the Guild, we can act as we like. Certainly, I don't intend to let them set us down anywhere they like. If we must, we will take over the ship."

"Why not?" Stoat chuckled. "If the main vessel is as small and old as I think it is, it only needs a crew of twelve experts to run it—and we are three know-nothings." But his eyes were alight with a quick hunter's delight, and Lahks laughed aloud, sure he knew more than enough about running a Guild ship and bringing a crew of Guildsmen to heel.

Chapter

18

The best-laid plans of mice and men, it is said, gang oft agley. And if droms are about, they gang agley more oft than usual.

As soon as the craft latched to the ship and the pressure locks opened, the drom, which had been sitting so quietly that everyone had almost forgotten it, charged through. It barreled right by the cargo handlers who had come to unload and, with an agility incredible in so huge a beast, scooted through the lock. Of what happened on the other side, Lahks and her companions were in ignorance. However, when the Cargomaster led them through the lock, they were all—including the Cargomaster himself—promptly felled by stunner blasts.

Lahks regained consciousness rapidly, but she neither moved nor opened her eyes. A little pseudopod grew out of her neck, divided in two, and squeezed her earlobe. Two things happened simultaneously. First, all Lahks' electronic equipment began to sing. Obviously there were "Watchers" and "Listeners" of every variety spying on them. Second, there was a muffled sound of revulsion from an area off to her right.

Although she did not wish to betray her consciousness, Lahks could not allow a stranger to tell the tale of that pseudopod. Unfortunately, Guildsmen were well trained. The sound had been so low and brief that Lahks could not locate the man without opening her eyes. Hoping that the Watchers would record only gross movement, Lahks let her eyes slide down her right cheek and open. She saw a crewman, green and retching with horror, and heard a low smothered chuckle. With flickering rapidity her hand turned: out of the palm a tiny sliver flew; the crewman collapsed, dropping the knife he had been about to use to the floor; Lahks' hand was in its original position before the crewman had started to fall. Safe in the curve of her neck and the shadow of her cheek, Lahks' eyes sat up and looked around brightly. The chuckle must have been from Stoat.

Very soon she spotted him. His whole body, including cheeks and lips, was flaccid with apparent unconsciousness, but one eye—as is common in unconscious people—was open a slit. Out of that slit, however, the eye regarded Lahks with lively intelligence. Well, at least she and Stoat were awake. Now they needed a way to communicate that would not be recorded by the spy eyes and ears around them. Lahks had just started to blink basic Guild dit-dat code when a tremendous hubbub could be heard coming down the corridor. She snapped her eyes back into place and closed them.

Although she had known the felling of the young Guildsman would be recorded, she had hoped there would be a few amin before anyone came to investigate. Actually, she had not been much concerned. The sliver would have dissolved, leaving no mark; she and her companions, limp and unconscious, could not be implicated. One or even a few men might come to investigate, yes, but why the shouting, the hiss of blasters, the sizzle of metal touched by laser? Mutiny?

Just as Lahks' agile mind seized on a method of turning such an event in their favor, the true cause of the disorder revealed itself. With the screech of metal tortured by a substance infinitely harder than any known, a long dent appeared near the door.

"Holy Yahweh! Here comes the rescue squad again!" Stoat exclaimed, abandoning any attempt to seem unconscious and sitting up. He followed up with what was rapidly becoming his favorite remark, "Damned droms."

Lahks, too, had sprung to life the moment it was apparent that the drom was set on getting them out. She rolled both Shom and Fanny under their respective bunks. It was little enough cover, but the best available. Stoat, however, instead of coming to help, shook his head at her.

"They will not kill us now. They will want to find out how to control the drom first."

"When they do find out," Lahks said sarcastically, "I wish they would tell me."

The cries in the corridor had resolved themselves from shrieks and shouts of fear and fury into one commanding voice. "Open the door! Open the door before that thing goes through the wall!"

There was a fumbling at the lock, as if a very fearful hand was trying to hurry. Another screech heralded the appearance of a narrow slit in the wall. A third would undoubtedly enlarge the gap so that the room would be useless as a prison—if it was not already. The fumbling grew more frantic. Lahks and Stoat braced themselves to jump or dodge as necessity demanded. The door gave, there was a shout of alarm, and a grinning reptilian head thrust through. Since the bulk of the drom blocked the doorway completely, there was no need for any immediate defensive action. Of course, it was also impossible for them to get out, so there was not much opportunity for offensive action, either. In fact, if the drom did not move, they were as effectively imprisoned now as before.

"Stoat," Lahks murmured sufficiently low so that the continuing hubbub in the corridor would screen their voices, "if they want to know why we recovered so fast, I carry a sonic shield—a new 'Trade' invention. Why did you recover so fast?"

Stoat's reply was pitched to be equally indistinguishable to the detection devices. "Master is proof against most sonic ranges. They'll want the device."

"I'll tell them it's personnel-coded. That will cover the mess of melted stuff. There's enough in it to look good."

"Yes, well, it will be helpful if and when we get out. That drom seems permanently planted. And what do we do when we get out?"

"Where is Control?"

"If this is the brig, there is nothing but cargo and reaction chambers below us. Everything else is above, and at the very top is Control."

"Probably too far," Lahks remarked, "unless we go under escort. If we allow them to capture us, where will they take us?"

"Usually to interrogation rooms, also at this level, but with the drom taking down walls..."

"Stoat," Lahks interrupted suddenly, her eyes widening, "if the drom came in on the cargo level, how did it get up the companionway? It wouldn't fit."

Stoat's mouth opened, shut with lips thinned, and then he spoke sharply. "How did you get out of the food slot? And that is equally irrelevant to what we must do now."

Lahks cocked her head. Stoat was never sharp when she introduced puzzles to him. They were all that added savor to a life so long that all experiences except death itself became familiar. The sharpness then must be generated by some internal struggle, and that could only be concerned with their present situation.

"You have a way, then, to bend this ship to your command?"

There was a silence while the dark eyes that ordinarily showed only a feral eagerness become shadowed with memory. "There is a way. Whoever else can endure revolution, a Guildmaster cannot. What is more, a Guildmaster may not wish to be known as such when he enters a particular situation. Thus Guildsmen are all imprinted to respond with protection and obedience to a certain code."

He was about to add something when the expletives and sounds of activity in the corridor took on a new tone. Lahks' lips twitched. "They are trying to move the drom by force. Since we have time, tell me what prevents a Guildmaster from forming a private army to take over from all other Guildmasters."

"Two things. The imprinting works only in the reasonable proximity of the Guildmaster. I can control this ship, these men, but nothing more. The second fail-safe is in the Guildmaster. When the imprinting for obedience is removed, as it must be to permit a Master to function, it is replaced by an imprinting that inhibits any action that will harm the Guild as a whole. That I still have, you know. I cannot move against the good of the Guild."

"Then is it possible to take over the ship? Will I have to block you, too?"

"No. This Captain intends to violate a Guild Deal. If I prevent him—since you intend to keep the Deal—I am acting in the best interests of the Guild. That such action also suits my private purposes is irrelevant."

Lahks looked at him for a moment and shook her head. "It is

too easy. Nothing could be so simple as the speaking of a few words. I suppose your code is secret?"

"No. It is, according to the sem-psychs, impossible to remember the sounds without deep conditioning. Actually, I do not remember them. I remember a mnemonic code. When I speak that aloud, it permits me to pronounce the sounds of the Master's code. But that is not the difficulty. If..."

Stoat's voice checked suddenly as the drom removed its head from the door to look over its shoulder reproachfully. Lahks had no idea what the crewmen were doing to it, but she and Stoat promptly fell to the floor and took cover in the least accessible corner.

"If I say those words," Stoat muttered hastily, "the Guild will hunt us to the end of the universe. And we are not hard to identify—a gorl, an idiot, a woman, and me. They know the number of Masters and where those Masters are. A stray being who knows the code..."

He did not need to finish. Lahks knew what he said was true and knew that it was impossible to brainwash the entire crew. They had to get to the Captain. Stoat could use the Master's code on him and Lahks could, she hoped, wipe the incident from his memory. The Cargomaster was already committed to the purpose she desired, and it was those two who controlled the ship.

A new outburst of obscenities from the corridor and the return of the drom's benign, if bemused, gaze to them indicated that the attempts to remove it had failed. "In your list," Lahks remarked dryly, "you forgot to mention the drom. It seems permanently attached."

Stoat smiled in acknowledgment, but his head was cocked toward the corridor. "I think the officer is acknowledging defeat," he murmured right into her ear. "Probably he will leave a couple of men on guard to give warning if the drom moves. That will be our chance."

"If the drom will let us out."

An expressive shrug was the only reply Lahks received, and she grinned, guessing the "damned drom" litany that must be going through Stoat's mind. Both knew their movements were probably monitored. As soon as they acted to escape, whether the drom moved or not, men would be alerted. They would have,

163

at best, a few amin to subdue the guards in the corridor. Hiding thereafter would be impossible if the drom followed them. Lahks was tempted to say "damned drom" herself, but Stoat said he knew the ship type, and she was willing to trust herself to his expertise.

They remained crouched in their corner, listening. Soon enough it was apparent that two men had been left on guard. Lahks could see Stoat eyeing the knife the Guildsman had dropped and gauging the distance. When the muscles of his jaw and throat tensed in preparation for the leap, Lahks threw the entire force of her will against the drom. "Out," she demanded silently. "We want out."

Stoat leaped, checking for a flicker of time to scoop up the knife so that Lahks, who had started to move a fraction of a sec later, arrived at the drom-blocked doorway at the same instant he did. Both truly expected to crash into the immovable creature. Although their minds urged them forward, the self-defensive mechanism of their bodies tensed against the impact. Therefore, when they arrived and the drom was not there, each exploded into the corridor with an unbalanced reel that could defy the finest marksman.

Although they fortunately reeled in opposite directions so that they did not collide and knock each other down, the situation was already well out of hand in other ways. On Stoat's side, the guard was tearing down the corridor shouting a warning. On Lahks' side, the drom, grinning and bobbing benignly, completely shielded the Guildsman from her lethal intentions.

Wasting no time in vain regrets, imprecations against droms, or attempts to get at the Guildsman, Stoat moved across the corridor and a few meters down it in the direction the guard had fled. Then he began feeling at the seams in the metal. In moments he breathed a sigh of relief and blessed the ancient ship as he found what he wanted. As he worked the service panel free, Lahks slipped past him. He had only to squeeze through himself and slam it shut. Their escape route would be obvious, but for the moment they were free of both Guildsmen and drom.

"How do we get to the Captain?" Lahks asked, flattening herself against the wall to let Stoat pass.

"I don't. You do. No service section goes to Control.

Control is completely separate, except for the air ducts. You'll have to make like a snake again to get through those."

As he spoke he moved swiftly forward and gestured Lahks upward. She scrambled up the hand- and foot-hold ladder, wondering where to stop. That question answered itself when the well ended in another service passage. Stoat's hand touched Lahks' right ankle and, obediently, she turned right again, flattening herself so he could pass. Some yards down the passage, he paused to place his ear against the wall. Lahks shook her head, then fingered the top of her ear to activate a sound magnifier. Shortly her hand went up in the null sign. Stoat fingered the studs and opened the panel. Here Lahks' equipment indicated no surveillance devices.

"Better than Engineering," Stoat commented softly. "It's easier to hide in the vegetation, if we have to, and they can't use gas on us because it would get into the air-concentrating equipment. You'll have to get the Captain here alone."

Lahks grinned. Stoat needed a little reeducation. Although a Guardian was competent to make the majority of the people of a nation or even of a whole planet act in a predetermined pattern, there was no guarantee she could bend a single man to her will without the use of drugs. The mass mind was low and brutal, the mass psychology simplistic in the extreme. An individual, on the other hand, even a low and brutal one, had a most complex psychology and a most devious mind. The reactions of any individual could not be planned for and predicted. However, this was not the moment for clarifying Stoat's notions.

After Stoat explained the duct system, Lahks wasted no time. She shed her clothing and crawled into the duct pointed out, elongating as she went. She wondered briefly whether there were any intelligent snake people, making a mental note to find out and take lessons in abdominal crawling. It was obviously a finer art and a far more useful method of locomotion than she had realized in the past. In a few moments, when Stoat had reconnected the duct to the blower, she was helped along by a strong tail wind.

To rise a level, Lahks had to stretch almost into a thread. At one time she felt as if the weight of body trailing behind her would snap her in two. She was tempted again to try a mist form, but again she feared the air currents would disperse her particles too widely. Obviously, she had not learned all the Changelings knew. It would definitely be necessary to take lessons from them too.

Another level up. Lahks was grateful for the high oxygen concentration in the air duct. Gasping for breath with lungs extended into threads (if she had lungs) would have been a problem. Finally a grating. Lahks moved her eyes to the most forward part of her and peered through.

The ship, as Stoat had predicted, was old and mostly not automatic. A man sat at the com console, another at the helm, a third at internal control, and a fourth at armament. For a mercy, the Captain was in the command chair. Lahks had wondered, if he was not there, how she would recognize him. Not that knowing her man did her much good. With five of them in the room, it would be impossible to deal with the Captain there. Helmsman and weaponeer were turned toward the com and con consoles, and the Captain was frowning.

"What do you mean, it disappeared?" he snarled. "Nothing that size can disappear."

The drom, Lahks thought, that idiot drom! The Power alone knew what it would do next—if it had enough mind for the Power to read. She did not take her eyes from the Captain, however, and her attention was rewarded. As the com officer spoke urgently into his instrument, the Captain cast his eyes around the room in an exasperated search for a spark of reason. Promptly Lahks extruded a delightfully feminine finger through the grate and beckoned enticingly.

The Captain's eyes fixed; his mouth opened. Lahks beckoned again, then withdrew her finger. The Captain stared, transfixed. He knew there was no woman in that duct. In fact, aside from a snake, it was impossible for any moderate-sized creature to be in there. He withdrew his eyes with determination and listened to the report his com officer was making on the search for the escaped prisoners. Nothing needing his attention had come up, however, and his eyes irresistibly returned to the duct.

This time Lahks extruded two fingers under his fascinated gaze. First she beckoned, and then she made the sign used in Transit bases by whores to solicit trade. The Captain's head jerked away. Then he rose suddenly and walked over to the air duct. Surprised, the men turned to watch, but Lahks had withdrawn her fingers as soon as the other men turned.

"Give me a light," the Captain commanded harshly.

Puzzlement showed on all faces as the weaponeer proffered a handlight. The expression deepened as the Captain rose on tiptoes and pressed the light against the grid. Lahks flattened herself and produced a skin with a dull metallic sheen so that, aside from a slight constriction, the duct looked just as usual.

"Something wrong, Captain?" the con officer asked uneasily, aware, that the air system had previously shown a red malfunction flicker. It had been so brief and had corrected itself so quickly that, in view of all the other things happening, the con officer had not mentioned it. The scowl the Captain turned on him did not encourage him to confess, particularly as the system showed green now.

The moment the Captain's head turned, Lahks tickled his cheek and whispered, "I like you. Come be with me," in her most dulcet tones.

Captains of Guild ships—especially those who consider betraying the Guild—are not timid men. The consciousness of intended betrayal tenses the nerves, however, and the incomprehensible antics of droms are scarcely a calming influence. When a man under severe tension begins to hear and see things that he knows are not there, he may be pardoned for suspecting that something is wrong with him.

The Captain backed away from the air duct, controlling his expression with an effort. He made an obscene comment about the living cargo his Cargomaster had seen fit to infest his ship with, added that he could be contacted in his quarters any time some helpful information turned up, and left the Control room.

Lahks had departed as soon as he stated his destination. Down was easy, and the path through the ducts was not long. She had oozed through the grating, resumed her normal form, and was behind the door when he entered his room. A dose of hypnotics turned him into an obedient mummy. Lahks sighed with relief—unfortunately a bit prematurely, because no sooner did she get the door closed than the com unit announced that one of the prisoners remaining in the brig was stirring and asked for instructions.

Had Lahks been given to temper tantrums, she would have thrown herself on the floor and roared. She dared not give the Captain the antidote, camouflage herself, and let him answer the com call, because in the temper he was in there was a chance he might order Fanny and Shom to be killed. It was not very likely, but it was possible. Moreover, what was most likely was that he would order them to be "questioned." She had intended to fix a hypnotic suggestion into his mind that the Captain must come alone to Hydroponics and leave it to him to explain why if he met anyone. She herself intended to return by the way she had come.

Now she could not leave him on his own at all. The hypnotic suggestion would probably be strong enough to get him to Hydroponics before he went anywhere else, but he would certainly give instructions about Fanny and Shom as soon as he heard the com call. She would have to change into a crewman, which was easy enough, but without a stitch of clothing... Lahks spared herself an exasperated thought as to why adjustable clothing could not be developed, then thought of the forms she had been taking recently and grinned.

Then the com repeated the message and requested, a little anxiously, that the Captain reply. There was no longer a moment to spare. The men in Control would know the Captain must have reached his quarters by now. Already alerted by what they felt was odd behavior, they would send someone to look for him if he did not soon reply. Lahks took on Stoat's face, enlarged herself to the Captain's size, dragged coveralls from his wardrobe, and slipped into them while giving her instructions. She could only hope that with the insignia-bearing collar turned under and the sleeves rolled up, no one would realize she was wearing the Captain's clothes.

One advantage Lahks was counting upon was the Captain's bad temper. She assumed that the ordinary ship's grapevine had already spread the word and that crewmen or officers would not take a chance on probing the somewhat wooden scowl she had fixed on his features. She had chosen Stoat's face because the crew, being small, would all know each other. A stranger who appeared on the ship in the midst of this turmoil would be an immediate target for suspicion, if not direct attack. As a final precaution, she had the Captain draw his weapon so that she/he would appear to be a prisoner.

The precautions Lahks had taken were certainly in order. The antics of the drom and the escape of two prisoners had stirred the crew like sticks poking into a hornet's nest. Everyone off watch seemed to be running around the corridors, and most of those on watch were peering out of the opened doors of their stations. The com plaintively repeated its information and requested that the Captain reply.

They were no sooner out the door than a young crewman running down the corridor skidded to a halt. "Captain..." he began.

"Later," the Captain said, sounding to Lahks horribly like a recording of her own voice. "Tell com to shut up."

That was undoubtedly not the usual procedure. The young crewman looked confused, glancing from the weapon to Stoat/Lahks to the Captain, but the scowl cowed him enough to make him back off down the corridor. He turned at the corner and ran, probably to seek advice from a higher authority, but fortunately the distance to Hydroponics was short enough so that they were not accosted again. Nonetheless, if they were not out of Ponics in a very few amin indeed, the entire crew would soon be in there with them. Lahks concentrated on compressing her instructions into the fewest possible words and readied the antidote.

The trick was to condition the Captain to forget that Stoat had used the Master's code after they had left the ship. Lahks was by no means sure that the hypnotic she had could be used in that fashion, particularly when she did not have sufficient time to reinforce the conditioning by repetition. If it did not work, all four of them were as good as dead, because the entire resources of the Guild would be turned upon them—and the resources of the Guild as a whole made even those of the Guardians insignificant.

As they came through the door, Lahks told the Captain to holster the weapon and told him he was incapable of using it for five amin. Then she began her brainwashing spiel. Her time sense ticked away the secs. At three-amin-fifty, she signaled Stoat. Without the rustle of a leaf, he was there. She held up a hand, hit the Captain with the antidote, dropped her hand, and inside her head pushed a red button.

To all intents and purposes Lahks was now a datarec. She had no power of speech, movement, reason, or feeling, no physical senses or sensations beyond those necessary to record forever the sights, sounds, and personality of whomever spoke. The red button was dangerous, dangerous. What she saw and heard would be impressed indelibly far deeper than any mental process, down below the ego onto the id itself. If something damaging should happen, Lahks would wither and die— Changeling or no Changeling. Her safety valve was the black button, which had a timed relationship and a data relationship to the red. At a pause in the flow of data, the black button would go down automatically and release the red; the same would happen if data flowed for longer than a certain short time period.

The Captain, free of his mental paralysis, was reaching for his holstered weapon. The mnemonic code, a series of nonsense syllables, slid from Stoat's lips. His eyes glazed, and he then produced a series of sounds that Lahks could have sworn were impossible to human vocal chords. The Captain stiffened into momentary paralysis again. For a moment naked hate showed in his face, but the compulsion was too strong. He could not act against Stoat.

"You will keep your Deal," Stoat said. "My companions and I will keep ours—and perhaps you will achieve your original object, anyway. Think about it. You can make your private profit and still stay clear of the vengeance of the Guild."

The indweller had released the red button as soon as the noises stopped coming from Stoat. Lahks melted away, leaving the Captain's coveralls lying empty on the floor. Now she reappeared rather noisily, wearing her own face and clothing. The Captain swung nervously toward the sound, his hand again going to his holster.

"My companions—all of them—are under my protection," Stoat said sharply.

But the Captain had relaxed as soon as he saw Lahks, even before Stoat spoke. It was not she he was arming himself against.

"And the beast?" he asked. "It is also yours?"

Stoat and Lahks laughed in chorus. "It is its own," Stoat replied. "We do not know why it is here, but it will do no harm."

"The ship is well provided, but where will we find food and water for a creature that size?"

"I do not think it eats or drinks," Lahks said slowly.

"On Wumeera it took those compressed protein pellets," Stoat remarked doubtfully. He had seen it "recharging," of course, but it might need more than energy to survive.

"Perhaps it was just being polite," Lahks suggested. "Anyway . . ."

"Polite!" the Captain gasped in an outraged voice, and then he made a wordless gurgle compounded of alarm and exasperation.

Lahks and Stoat swung around so they could see what his bulging eyes had fastened upon. They were not surprised to find a grinning reptilian head with bobbing eyes nodding benignly at them from between the Ponics growth. Both laughed aloud.

"Do you realize," the Captain said with strained reserve, "that if it eats what grows in here, we will all die?" Then as the drom came forward to be closer, he gasped again. "How did it get up here?" he cried. "There is no shaft, no companionway it could pass through."

"We do not know!" Lahks and Stoat exclaimed in chorus.

With a twinkle in her eyes, Lahks continued, "Perhaps it oozes through the air ducts. It can change its shape."

Rage leaped anew into the Captain's eyes. He ground his teeth. "And it whispers lewd invitations in a woman's voice?" he grated.

Lahks lowered her lashes demurely over her dancing eyes. "I have never heard it make any sound, but it is obviously most attracted to you, Captain. Who knows what it can do when sufficiently inspired?"

There was a short silence, although Lahks and Stoat could imagine they heard a sizzling noise as the Captain damped down his erupting temper.

"Go ahead," Stoat remarked, grinning so that all his sharp teeth showed. "Go kick it if you like. It won't mind. It might lick you to show its appreciation of the notice you have taken of it. I have several broken toes I got that way, having spent some years on Wumeera."

Aside from clenching his fists, the Captain did not move. "You can have passenger cabins two and four," he said at last, in a voice markedly reminiscent of a man being garroted. "You may hope my conditioning will hold, if your hint of profit is not true, Master, but you can buy surety."

He waited, as if expecting Stoat to come up with two heartstones. "It will hold," Stoat said quietly but grimly. "Reward follows performance." Without another word the

Captain turned and left Ponics. Stoat cocked an appraising eye at Lahks and "tsk-tsked." "Lewd invitations," he said. "I am shocked."

Lahks giggled, but her attention was fixed on the drom. "I wonder how it does get from place to place."

"Teleports? How did the droms get into the middle of that desert when we needed them?"

"I have no idea, but if so, why did it take them a full day? Why weren't they there when we started to move the flyer?"

Staring at the grinning creature, they both sighed. This was one problem that was not going to elucidate itself—at least not until the drom wanted it elucidated, if ever. Meanwhile, they had better get Shom and Fanny moved to more comfortable quarters and recover their weapons and baggage.

When the brig door was opened, Shom was immediately visible; Fanny, however, was gone. The crewman who had unlocked the door uttered an unbelieving oath and stepped incautiously inside. As he cleared the door, a neatly twisted garrote caught him around the neck and he was whirled behind the door to be used as a shield.

"Easy, Fanny!" Stoat cried. "Don't kill him. We have made terms with the Guild."

"Come in," Fanny growled. "Close door."

It was a wise precaution, showing that Fanny was a worthy member of the team. Had Stoat and Lahks been prisoners, Stoat might have been forced to say what he did. They came in and Fanny slammed the door shut. Since both were smiling and neither made any move to avoid an attack, Fanny relaxed his grip on the crewman. He looked without favor at his victim, whose bulging eyes and purple complexion were slowly returning to normal.

"Maybe tear off arm as lesson?" Fanny asked hopefully.

"Now, now, don't be vindictive," Lahks protested. "They didn't do us any harm, really."

Fanny's eyes shifted significantly around the room. Lahks touched his arm, he thrust the still-dazed crewman into Stoat's arms, and they moved into the corridor.

"Spy eyes but no ears here," Lahks remarked softly, her lips scarcely moving. "We are buying our way free with an extra heartstone."

"Cheap—if believe is all have. Will?"

"I hope so. Anyway, I think they are anxious to get rid of us without killing us if they can. They don't want both the gorls and Trade after them, as well as the Guild. Besides, they know the drom won't let them imprison us." She gestured toward the dented wall. Fanny stared at it with disbelief for a moment, then vented his growling chuckle.

"Drom wants something," he said.

"Yes," Lahks agreed. "I think so, too. But, what? And how will it tell us?"

Again Fanny's fangs were bared in amusement. "Will find way. Sure of that."

Stoat and the scowling crewman emerged from the brig. "Will you carry Shom, Fanny?" Stoat asked. "I'll take the packs."

By common consent, Shom and Fanny were paired. They decided to keep Shom in his drugged sleep because he could not be awakened without returning his stone, and there was some chance that someone would notice what he had. As Stoat lifted his pack and that of Lahks, Fanny remarked that he would see if he was allowed to wander around the ship to test their degree of freedom.

"What heading?" he asked.

Although there was small chance of Fanny being allowed into the Control room, he might discover their intended direction by indirect means.

"The Deal was to take us to the nearest transshipment port," Lahks replied, "but considering the Captain's mood, we might end up at the outermost star of the rim."

"And what if the rim he heads for is the wrong direction?"

"Is there a wrong direction for you?" Lahks asked Stoat.

He stared at her, then smiled his sharp weasel grin. "Not for me, if you are headed there."

Lahks turned courteously to Fanny. "And for you, Prince? Is there some particular direction in which you wish to travel?"

The gorl exposed his tearing fangs. "Call Fanny. No more Prince. No more Clanmaster. Mad adventurer, instead. Anywhere good." A grumbling laugh shook him. "Go where drom wants. Should be fun."

Lahks cocked her head. "It might be at that," she agreed.

"And if what we guessed about the makers of the drom and the drom itself is true," she added, "the drom might lead us to Ghrey more directly than my 'knowledge' of his whereabouts. The drom has *very* direct methods of getting what it wants."

They all laughed and went out together, Fanny to prowl down the corridors, Stoat and Lahks to settle into the adjoining cabin. When Stoat had set the packs down, he turned to Lahks. His feral eyes were unusually peaceful, his expression uncertain and singularly defenseless.

"On Wumeera I offered you permanent Contract," he said softly. "You said then I should speak of it again when we were off-planet and I knew the full tale of your woes. Beldame, I no longer care what your woes or joys are or where your paths lead. I only know I wish to share all things with you." He put out his left hand, palm up. "Will you make Contract with me—for body *and* labor? Permanent may be a long time for us, but ..."

Lahks' hand was already on his, briefly palm to palm, and then in a tight clasp. "Permanent Contract without conditions for body and labor. Agreed." Her eyes, unshadowed and, for once, unsmiling, met his fully.

Stoat used her clasping hand to draw her to him. "It is very long since I have dared to love," he murmured.

Lahks lifted her face to his. "Whether we go to a transshipment point or to the rim, just now we have time—a few days."

"But a few days is an eternity to us," Stoat said gravely, "as an eternity must pass for us like a few days."

"Until forever, then." Lahks smiled as their lips met.

Bestselling Novels From POCKET BOOKS